NIGHT OF THE
COYOTE

a novel by
RON SCHWAB

Poor Coyote Press
PO Box 6105
Omaha, NE 68106
www.PoorCoyotePress.com

ISBN: 1-943421-03-X
ISBN-13: 978-1-943421-03-9

NIGHT OF THE COYOTE

1

STIFF GUSTS OF wind whipped at the mammoth cottonwood that ignored civilization's assault in the center of one of the two intersections on Lockwood's main street. The tree's branches trembled, and the rustling of its fragile leaves was the only sound in the little Wyoming town this June morning in 1875. Silent corpses, suspended by twin reatas from a sturdy limb that arched out from the tree's trunk, swayed with the rocking of the branch, and two dark shadows danced like ghostly ballerinas on the dusty road.

A rider, sitting tall with military bearing in his Cheyenne saddle, reined in his Appaloosa gelding and tugged the brim of his low-crowned hat forward to ward off the glare of the mountain sunrise. His face was impassive, but his steel-gray eyes smoldered as he studied the grotesque scene.

Sioux, he guessed. But he could not tell from their dress or traditional tribal accoutrements, for they had been stripped naked, which somehow made their deaths more obscene. They were no more than boys, and the agony he read on the swollen, contorted faces left him weak. What terror, what incomprehensible fear they must have endured in those early moments of their lynching, before the rawhide ropes had either strangled them to death or mercifully snapped their necks.

Ethan Ramsey dug into his pocket and pulled out his jackknife, opened it and nudged his horse toward the swinging bodies. The horse was skittish and whinnied nervously as they approached the Indian youths. "Easy, Patch," Ethan said as he stroked the horse gently on the neck. "Easy, boy."

At the sound of his rider's voice, the horse steadied and Ethan leaned away from the saddle, stretching to his limit as he worked the razor-edged knife through the rope strands. Suddenly, the first rope gave way, and the young man's body dropped like a sack of grain to the ground. In a few moments, the other joined his companion. Without so much as a glance at their bodies, Ethan turned the horse away and headed at a slow gait toward the livery stable a block further down the road.

Dismounting in front of Fletcher's Livery, he brushed haphazardly at the dust that frosted his tailored gabardine suit and then led the Appaloosa through the open doors of the barn.

"Enos," he called.

"Back here, Ethan," came a gravelly voice from the darkness at the rear of the barn. Grizzled Enos Fletcher emerged from behind one of the stalls and hobbled toward Ethan. The silver-bearded man spat a wad of brown chewing tobacco before he spoke. "You don't look none too cheerful this mornin', Ethan," he said matter-of-factly, as he accepted the horse's reins.

"What happened, Enos?"

"I figured you seen 'em when you come in. Ain't too appetizin', huh?" The old man spat again and shook his head gloomily from side to side. "Goddamned awful, Ethan, that's what it is. Goddamned awful. And there's gonna be hell to pay."

"You didn't answer my question—what happened?"

"Well, Jake Harper's got burned out last night. Him and his girl, slaughtered like butcher hogs and burned to a crisp, they say. Talk is they saw the fire from the Webb place and some hands went over to have a look-see. But it was too late. They could see it was injun work so they sent a man to town to fetch the sheriff. Will Bridges is in Cheyenne, so that half-witted deputy of his, Rube Tatnall, went along to the Harper place. You know Rube. He don't know horseshit from wild honey."

"That doesn't explain the Sioux boys out on the street."

"Well, old Rube rides on out, and after he sees the mess, decides he's gonna round up a posse and swears in the Circle W wranglers on the spot. As near as they could tell, there couldn't have been many injuns at the Harper place, so him and his so-called posse took off like bats out of hell. If you ask me, he didn't expect to find nothin'. But damned if they didn't come upon these young bucks a few miles west of the Harper place—three of 'em, just sitting there by the fire, like nothin' ever happened. Guess they didn't even try to make a break for it first. Anyhow, they hog-tied them and headed back to town to toss 'em in jail till Will got back—that's what Rube says, anyways. On the way, though, some of the boys started hitting the bottle a bit and talkin' pretty brave. Reckoned they could save the county the money of a trial and just string the bucks up right away."

"You said there were three boys, Enos. What happened to the third?"

"Well, only two of them made it to town. One broke his pony loose from the bunch and high-tailed it out before they got to town. Old Rube, he wasn't about to go after the injun hisself . . . he's yellar as a gold nugget . . . and the others was so liquored up by that time, they wasn't much help. Anyhow, they never got as far as the jail. You seen what happened. They say old Rube didn't even try to stop them. Just stood there with his hands in his pocket playin' with his pecker. The others stripped the injuns bare-ass naked. Then, as one fellar said, gave them baths in the water troughs and hung 'em up to dry."

"None of it adds up," Ethan said, "and even if it did, those boys were murdered. When's Will Bridges coming back?"

"Day after tomorrow, and he'll be mad as a stirred-up hornet. If I was Rube Tatnall, I don't think I'd stick around these parts."

"Where's Rube now?"

"Ain't seen hide nor hair of him this morning, but I expect he'll show up over to the sheriff's office sooner or later. He usually leaves his horse off here. Want me to let you know when he shows?"

"I'd appreciate it. I'd like you to do something else, too."

Fletcher squinted one eye and looked up at the taller man. "And what might that be?" he asked suspiciously.

"I'm already late for an appointment and I'd like to get those bodies off the street. Would you check with George Caldwell and see if he can pick them up? Maybe keep them at his place until the sheriff decides what to do?"

"He won't do it," the old man said flatly. "I already mentioned it when he was in here. He says nobody'd want to be buried by an undertaker who worked on redskins. Besides, he's got a load of furniture coming in today."

Ethan knew it would be hopeless to argue with George Caldwell who ran Lockwood Funerals & Furniture, as well as half dozen other enterprises out of the same frame business building. Caldwell posed as a pious, God-fearing man, yet made no move without serious contemplation of the potential consequences to his business interests. It mattered not that he had no competition in the little community.

"All right," Ethan said. "What about you, Enos? Can you get a buckboard down there and get them off the street and covered up?"

"I don't know about that," Fletcher said skeptically. "By whose authority?"

"Mine. If Rube Tatnall says anything, send him over to me."

"You ain't the law."

"I'm a lawyer, and that's about as close as this town's got to law right now. And don't worry, I'll foot the bill for your trouble."

Fletcher's eyes brightened noticeably. "Well, I suppose I can take care of it as soon as my stable boy gets back. But what do I do with them?"

"Just bring them back here for now. I'll think of something. I'll be responsible."

Fletcher shrugged. "It's your money. Damned fool way to spend it, if you ask me."

2

ETHAN LEANED FORWARD at his desk and thumbed through the hornbook, gazing at the fine print as he flipped the pages but not seeing what was written there. He supposed he should draft Mrs. Thomsen's will, for the elderly widow had indicated before her departure a few minutes earlier that she was eager to have her new will completed. He knew that his sole competitor, Charley Langdon, had prepared Mrs. Thomsen's previous will; it would be just his luck that Effie Thomsen would die before she signed the new one, and crafty old Charley would get to probate the estate. And Effie Thomsen had land holdings that would make probate worth a lawyer's while.

But his thoughts kept returning to the hangings. He had seen death in his 30 years, rendered his share of it in the three years he served as Chief of Scouts at Fort Laramie. But this was 1875 and the Sioux bands that occupied this part of Wyoming had been at peace since Spotted Tail, when their Chief had signed the treaty of 1868 at Fort Laramie. He could not quite swallow the notion that Sioux boys had murdered the Harpers. He had a gut feeling that told him that the unfortunate boys whose lives had been so brutally snuffed out on the main street the night before had had nothing to do with the killings. It was not only the obvious youth of the lynching victims that triggered his doubts. What Sioux male, young or old, would have carried out such a raid, and then set up camp a few miles away to await capture?

They were two days' hard ride from Fort Laramie, and Lockwood was an island of semi-civilization at the base of the Laramie Range of the Rocky Mountains. The town was dangerously vulnerable to Sioux attack, and a full-scale uprising could wipe out the town and the surrounding ranches in a matter of a few days. If the Sioux were not on the warpath now, word of the hangings could set off a major Indian war. Ethan seethed at the stupidity and barbarism of the men who had murdered the Indian boys in the name of justice.

The door to Ethan's office opened and his secretary came in. Her eyebrows were arched high and her nose uplifted like she smelled something unpleasant. Ethan wondered if he had horse manure on his boots but discarded that notion, reminding himself that she acted that way half the time. She was competent and efficient as a secretary, but she tended to be quarrelsome, and he was frequently irritated by her ability to intimidate him. Katherine Wyeth had been something of an institution in the office before he had commenced reading law with Horace Weatherby a few years earlier. After Ethan passed the bar, Weatherby had been in a hurry to sell his practice and move on, and Ethan had inherited Miss Wyeth in the process. He had wondered more than once whether his predecessor had headed for California to elude his problems with the bottle or to escape Miss Wyeth.

Hell, what could he do? Charley Langdon's wife was Charley's secretary, and other legal secretaries just weren't to be had in Lockwood, Wyoming. Besides, Katherine Wyeth was dedicated. She had to be a few years past child-bearing age by now, so it seemed unlikely someone would marry her and spirit her away.

"Mr. Ramsey?" Miss Wyeth said.

"What is it, Miss Wyeth?"

"There's a . . . uh . . . a young woman here to see you. I told her you were busy, but she's very persistent. She insists she's going to stay in the office until you see her."

"Well, I suggest you send her in. I'm not all that busy anyway, Miss Wyeth."

It annoyed him that Miss Wyeth always took it upon herself to determine whether or not he was too busy to see a prospective client. Often he felt like he was working for her instead of vice versa.

Miss Wyeth stood by the door, stiff and unmoving, like a statue, her thin lips pursed. "I said you could send her in, Miss Wyeth."

She appeared deaf to his instructions. "There's something else, Mr. Ramsey. The woman dresses like she's from the Quaker school . . . but I'm certain she's an Indian."

"So?"

"Well, we've never represented," she hesitated, "those kind of . . . people in this office."

He fought the urge to get out of his chair and kick the pompous woman in the butt. "Miss Wyeth," he said, enunciating his words slowly and clearly, "I will represent anyone who can pay a fee, and some who cannot, if it suits me. I think it behooves both of us to see that I don't starve out of this town. So, if you don't mind, send in my client . . . please."

Miss Wyeth shot him a killing glare and did an about face, opened the door and marched out of the office, her skirt swishing loudly. "Miss dePaul," came Miss Wyeth's voice from the reception room, "Mr. Ramsey says he can see you for just a few minutes."

Ethan stood when his visitor entered the room and closed the door softly behind her. She wore a drab, gray dress and matching bonnet, and her simple attire belied the fact that she had to be the most stunning woman he had ever seen. Tall for her race, the woman, who was perhaps a half dozen years younger than himself, hesitated a moment, appraising him with dark, intelligent eyes before she approached his desk with her hand extended.

"Mr. Ramsey, I am Skye dePaul. Thank you for seeing me . . . although I really did not give you much choice."

"I am pleased to meet you, Miss dePaul. Won't you be seated?"

Skye dePaul moved easily into one of the oak chairs in front of Ethan's desk. He stared at her in spite of himself, for Lockwood was not over-populated with young women, and, as the town's most eligible bachelor, he had encountered none who could hold a candle to this woman's physical beauty—smooth, bronzed skin; long, silky black hair; delicate features. He speculated that there was a lithe, full figure beneath her cotton dress.

"I am not a horse," Skye dePaul said.

He could feel the hot crimson spreading over his cheeks and down the back of his neck. He was both embarrassed and angered by her remark, although he detected neither mischief nor bitterness in her voice.

"I'm not certain I know what you mean," Ethan replied, knowing exactly what she meant. He gathered his composure quickly, "I assume you have some business with me this morning, Miss dePaul."

"Perhaps. I need a lawyer, one with your background . . . if I decide you are suitable for the job I have in mind."

"Well, then, I suggest we get right to the point, Miss dePaul. I, too, have to decide whether you and your job are suitable for me," he replied sardonically.

This meeting was going to be a waste of both of their times. They were off on the wrong foot, approaching each other like two feisty bobcats, wary and guarded, spoiling for a fight.

"Mr. Ramsey," she said, "I have lived in your community for slightly over one year. I am a teacher at the Pennock School."

"I assumed as much from your dress."

"I am a Quaker, Mr. Ramsey. We prefer to be called Friends. I am also a half-breed. My mother is Brule Sioux; my father was French. Does that bother you?"

"I think it bothers you," he said. "If you want to call yourself a half-breed, then I guess I'm one, too. My father was Scotch and my mother, Swiss. And as for you being a Quaker, I could not care less. I'm a lawyer who would like to help you with your legal problem . . . if I am suitable."

Her face was emotionless and he could read nothing into the cool eyes which still seemed to be evaluating him.

"Mr. Ramsey, I understand you were responsible for removing the bodies of the Sioux boys off the street this morning. I thank you for that."

Ethan shrugged, deciding he would keep his mouth shut while he figured out how to converse with this woman.

Miss dePaul continued. "The boys' names were Screeching Hawk and Raven Eyes. They were of my mother's village. They could not have been more than 16 years old. There was another with them who escaped."

"That's what I was told at the stable."

"The boy who got away is my cousin, Bear Killer. He came to our dormitory last night and tapped on my window. He told me what had happened and then rode away to his village. Bear Killer's father, Lame Buffalo, is Chief of the village and the brother of my mother, Singing Lark. He is a man of honor, but he has not always agreed with Spotted Tail's efforts to make peace with the white man. He is still a relatively young man and capable of counting many coups before he dies. When Bear Killer tells him about the death of his friends, my uncle will call for a war council."

"I'm not surprised," Ethan said. "There could be a lot of people who die because of what happened last night. But I don't see what I can do about it."

"I have heard of you before, Mr. Ramsey. They talked of you in my uncle's village when I visited there. You were Chief of Scouts at Fort Laramie. You were not loved by our tribe. You were said to be like a puma, wily and silent in your pursuit, springing from nowhere at the most unexpected times to bring death to our people. But you were respected as a warrior, and it was said that you could be trusted, that you killed as a warrior killed. Because war demanded it, not for the love of killing. Last night, after Bear Killer departed, I left the dormitory and walked alone into the hills. It was quiet, like death. But suddenly, as I walked, the coyotes began to howl in the woods, first one, then another in answer, until there was a chorus of them. And just as suddenly, they stopped. At that moment, your name came to my mind. I had never seen you before this morning, but I knew you were a lawyer in this town and was aware what you had done before. I took it for a sign."

Ethan was tempted to comment that he thought it a bit unusual for a Quaker to believe in such signs. "I've never had a client referred by a coyote before," he said, "but I'm not in a position to be choosy about my referrals."

"Spare me your sad attempts at humor, Mr. Ramsey. I want to retain your services, not your wit."

Did the woman ever smile? She must be a sourpuss for a teacher. "I'm listening," Ethan said.

"I want to return the bodies of Screeching Hawk and Raven Eyes to the village of Lame Buffalo. I would like you to help me do this. And, I want you to help me convince Lame Buffalo that Bear Killer must return with us, to stand trial, if necessary, for the murders of the Harper family. I will employ you to be Bear Killer's lawyer; but more importantly, I want you to assure Lame Buffalo that the real killers will be found and brought to justice."

Ethan shook his head in disbelief. "You don't expect much."

"I am asking you only to try. I think Lame Buffalo can be persuaded to give us time; he will not believe that the murderers of Screeching Hawk and Raven Eyes are also subject to the white man's laws. But he would like to see us fail to prove it. Time enough later for revenge. He will be very reluctant to let Bear Killer return with us, but I do not think we will get any cooperation out of the white authorities unless he does. Bear Killer is known in this area, and I have heard that he was identified by one of the men last night."

"When I took up law, I thought I picked a nice, safe occupation. But just for the sake of argument, let's say I get to Lame Buffalo's village without getting my scalp lifted. I can't lie to him; I can't guarantee Bear Killer's safety. Sheriff Bridges is a good man, and I think we could give the boy protection once we got him back to Lockwood. But a jury's another thing. The people in the county will be enflamed by that time, and I don't know if we can get an impartial jury, whether I could win the case. We're assuming, of course, that Bear Killer and his friends were innocent."

"You think so, do you not?" she asked bluntly.

"Well, yes. Even if the boys had taken some crazy notion to go on the warpath, they wouldn't have been stupid enough to make camp a few miles from where they massacred a family. They would have kept on the move all night and all the next day. And the boys I saw had not been painted for war; the lynch mob couldn't have washed off all signs of it. If Sioux, or warriors from any other tribe did it, those boys weren't very likely among them. But to find out who did it is another thing. The odds are against anybody in that mob getting more than a slap on the wrist; I don't think Lame Buffalo is going to be happy with the white man's justice."

"Will you take the job?"

"I don't know."

"I am not asking you to crusade for a cause, Mr. Ramsey. I can pay your fees. My father was a merchant in Cheyenne; he knew that when he died my mother would return to her own people. I was his only child, and he left his modest estate to me. I am not wealthy, but I have enough to pay your fees. I can draw a draft on a Cheyenne bank for your retainer today. Would two hundred dollars be adequate? You can present a bill when further fees are in order."

"You've hired yourself a lawyer, Miss dePaul . . . and an Indian scout and whatever else it is I'm going to be." Fees of this magnitude were rare as ivory in Lockwood, Wyoming.

"Good. I shall give the draft to your secretary when I leave."

Skye dePaul had evidently not been blind to Miss Wyeth's prejudice. In her own way, the French-Sioux woman was going to take a little of Miss Wyeth's scalp before her departure. He hoped he could get a glimpse of Miss Wyeth's face when the "lowly Indian woman" handed her the draft.

"Miss dePaul, before you leave, I'll need some instructions. Those boys have already been dead half a day. I've got some things to tend to before I leave town, but I'd better get on my way to Lame Buffalo's village by mid-afternoon. My guess is I'll be at least two nights on the trail. I know the country, but you'll have to give me some idea where to find the village."

"You must not have heard me, Mr. Ramsey. I will be going with you. Otherwise, it is doubtful you would get into the village alive. And if you did, Lame Buffalo would not even give you a hearing if you rode into the village alone."

"I can appreciate that, Miss dePaul, but this isn't going to be any boarding school outing, and your colleagues at the Pennock School might question the propriety of your heading into the mountains unchaperoned with a man."

"Mr. Ramsey, I have never cared for boarding school picnics, and as for the chaperone, the ladies at the school only know that I am taking a leave of absence. Certainly, I am not afraid to accompany you, because it would not disturb me greatly to cut your eyes out if you failed to behave like a gentleman."

She meant it, too. He could see it in her eyes. My God what kind of client had he taken on? She was crazy as hell.

"All right," he said. "I'll make arrangements for packing the bodies. I'll have to go out to my ranch and pick up some horses and gear and leave word with my partner. What about you? Do you have a horse?"

"No."

"I'll bring one."

"I would prefer something spirited."

"I thought so."

"Red Horse drove me here in the school's carriage. I shall purchase some supplies at Wilson's General Store, then return to the dormitory and change. Red Horse will help me haul the supplies out to the McWilliams Bridge, and I shall meet you there. Do you know the place?"

"About a mile west of the school. If you'll get the supplies, I should be there by . . . say three o'clock?"

"I will be waiting." She rose and extended her hand again. "Good day, Mr. Ramsey."

He took her hand. "Good day, Miss dePaul."

3

IT WAS AFTERNOON by the time Ethan pulled Enos Fletcher's rickety buckboard onto the narrow trail that branched off the main road and led to the Lazy R ranch buildings nestled a half mile into the foothills. Patch, tied to the rear of the buckboard, was nervous and skittish, spooked by the rancid smell of death that rose from the two blanket-covered corpses laid out in the wagon box. It was hot for early June in Wyoming, and flies swarmed and buzzed at his cargo in anticipation of a feast. The prospect of packing the bodies into the mountains for the better part of two days was not a pleasant one. It would be cooler at the higher elevations. Perhaps that would slow the deterioration of the corpses. Ethan was beginning to have second thoughts about the retainer he had accepted. Neither his client, nor her cause, was a popular one, and he could be permanently damaging the law practice he hoped to build in Lockwood.

Still, his office had not exactly overflowed with paying clients the past year, and the ranch was not close to carrying itself yet. Another mortgage payment would be due in September, and Skye dePaul, disagreeable and arrogant as she appeared to be, was able to pay his fees.

The woman. Now, there was a different breed of cat. In spite of her drab Quaker attire, Skye dePaul exuded a beauty that seemed at once gentle and untamed, and there was a naturalness to it, an innocent seductiveness, that set her apart from all other beautiful women he had known. And, undeniably, there was something about her that stirred a man's desire.

But there was also something cold and forbidding about her, and he had a hunch that her threat to kill or maim was more than bluff. Despite her aloofness and the mean streak that had surfaced, however, he had to concede she was a damn smart woman, obviously well-educated, and practical enough to apply what she had learned. At this point, he could barely hope for her friendship, but, nonetheless, she was an interesting woman and he was very curious about her.

As the wagon rattled into the ranch yard, his eyes scanned the corrals and barns for some sign of his partner, Ben Dobbs. Instinctively, he sensed that Ben was gone, that there was no human presence on the place.

He pulled the team to a stop near the hay barn that dominated the ranch's building site and then got down from the wagon and untied Patch, leading the big gelding to one of the corrals where he released the horse. "Take it easy a spell, Patch," he said. "You've got to go back to work in a while."

As he strode across the yard toward the weathered frame house, Ethan caught sight of a little whirlwind of dust that was working its way up the draw that nearly split the ranch from north to south. It was almost a mile away, and Ethan could see neither rider nor horse, but he could tell from the speed and tempo of the powdery shield that it was Ben Dobbs and his black mare.

Ben Dobbs had partnered with Ethan on the small ranch for two years now, and before that the old mountain man had scouted for the army out of Fort Laramie. It was in the army that Ethan and Ben had formed their fast friendship. Their business arrangement was a loose one. Ethan owned three sections that comprised the ranch—small by any standard—having made the down payment with the money squirreled away from his years of scouting for the army. He also owed the note and mortgage that a Cheyenne bank held against the ranch.

Ben had made the investment in the Hereford cattle that grazed the range, maintaining that he wanted no roots in the land, that a time would come when he would get the urge to drift on, and when that time came, Ethan could buy him out or they could sell enough cattle to settle the partnership.

Ethan waited in the ranch yard for his partner's arrival. Poor Ben. He was a relic from the past, nearer Indian than white in many ways. He was like a wild creature spawned from the mountains, constantly on the run from civilization. Ben was increasingly restless these days as Lockwood grew and new ranchers established themselves in the surrounding valleys. Calving season was just about over, and Ethan had a feeling Ben would not be around for another one.

Ben Dobbs rode in, his wide-brimmed Plainsman hat casting a dark shadow over his face. Ben was a good half foot shorter than Ethan's own six feet two inches, but his barrel-chest and powerful arms and shoulders gave him the appearance of a much larger man in the saddle. Closer to 70 than 60, Ben moved with the grace and ease of a man half his age. A black patch concealed Ben's naked left eye socket where Cheyenne torture had left its mark some years earlier. But when he dismounted in front of Ethan, his good eye was fastened appraisingly on the buckboard across the yard. The buckskin-clad man rubbed at the thick, gray stubble on his chin before he ambled up to Ethan. He said nothing, but the quizzical look on his face expressed his curiosity.

"They're Sioux, Ben," Ethan said, answering his partner's unspoken question. "Boys. They were lynched in town last night."

"Them jackasses looking for an injun war?"

"That's what it looks like, doesn't it?"

"You're goddamned right." Ben nodded toward the wagon. "You starting a collection or something?"

"Worse than that." He told Ben about Skye dePaul and the job he had agreed to take on. When he was finished, Ben stared at him in disbelief.

"There ain't no changin' your mind, is there?" the crusty old man asked.

"I've already made it up. I'll be pulling out this afternoon in an hour or so."

"Want me to ride along?"

"Why? You think I'm crazier than hell for doing it."

"Yep, but I've saved your scalp more than once."

"I won't deny that. But we'll be riding right into the middle of Lame Buffalo's camp. He'll either let us in or he won't, and once we get that far, your being along won't change the outcome. Besides, somebody's got to watch the ranch. And I've got something else I want you to check out while I'm gone."

"What's that?"

"I want you to go over to the Harper place, see what you can find out about how those people were killed. Look up Red

Horse, the Pawnee who's kind of a handyman over at the Quaker school. He might be able to give some help . . . especially if you need to do some digging."

"Digging?"

"Yeah. I understand the so-called posse buried the Harpers last night. I think somebody ought to take a look at the bodies, and Will Bridges won't be back for a few days. Rube's just hiding out trying to decide whether to cut and run. By the time anybody else makes an investigation, it may be too late to learn anything."

"Christ on a crutch. You always got a way of gettin' out of the messy jobs," Ben grumbled. "If there's shit to clean out of the barn, old Ben always gets stuck doing it. Now you got me robbing graves."

Ethan knew Ben would be happier if the task was his own idea, and decided to change his approach. "I'm sorry, Ben. It's not fair for me to pull you into this. Things could get pretty hot before this is over, and I wouldn't want to cause you any trouble. It might be better if you sort of stay neutral, sit this one out, maybe."

"You don't want my help?"

"I didn't say that. I'm just suggesting that maybe this isn't your fight."

"A man that straddles the fence usually gets sore balls," Ben growled.

"Well, it's up to you, Ben."

"Oh, what the hell. I'll find old Red Horse, and we'll mosey out that way before sundown. The grave diggin' though, that'll have to wait till after dark."

"Thanks, Ben. I appreciate it. Now, I've got to change and get my bedroll together. Uh, Ben . . . those Indian boys . . . I can't take them into the mountains in that buckboard."

Ben grimaced and squinted his good eye in displeasure. "Why, shit no. I'll get a couple of pack horses, wrap 'em up nice and pretty for you. Maybe even put ribbons on them."

"Thanks again."

"Think nothin' of it. I always wanted to be a goddamned undertaker." Ethan moved toward the house. Then he stopped and turned around to face Ben who had not budged an inch. "Something else I can do for you, Ethan?" Ben asked.

"Yeah. I'll need an extra packhorse for gear and food. And I want Razorback."

"Razorback? That half-broke stallion? What do you want him for?"

"Skye dePaul, the woman who's going with me. She needs a horse, too."

"You don't want that crazy stud horse for no woman."

"She said she likes a spirited horse."

"Old Razorback ain't just spirited, he's goddamn loco, that's what he is."

"Tell you what. Pick out one of the gentle mares, too. If our Miss dePaul can't handle Razorback, I'll leave him tied at the McWilliams Bridge. You can pick him up there when you go by the Quaker school to get Red Horse."

"Sounds to me like you're up to devilment with that woman."

"Just taking her at her word."

4

ETHAN CAUGHT SIGHT of the supplies stashed in the brush as he dismounted in front of the wooden bridge that spanned the clear creek. He stood quietly beside his Appaloosa searching the trees and undergrowth that lined the creek, seeking out Skye dePaul, whom he sensed was secreted there.

Then silently, like a cat, she emerged from a grove of aspen upstream and moved toward him. She looked more Indian than French now, Ethan observed, with her straight black hair tied back by a leather thong before it cascaded over her shoulders to the middle of her back. Her feet were clad in a pair of well-worn doeskin moccasins, and she wore a hip-length buckskin shirt that exposed an ample portion of the smooth brown skin of her neck and shoulders. The faded, denim trousers that clung to her legs and hips, which confirmed the curves he had earlier guessed would be there, were of the white man's world. He suspected that the bone-handled skinning knife sheathed at her side was more than decoration.

As Skye approached, she cast her eyes upward, squinting into the bright afternoon sun. "At least you are prompt, Mr. Ramsey. I like that."

"I try to be," he replied. "Were you hiding from someone?"

"I was just avoiding trouble. After last night, I would think it the better part of discretion for an Indian to stay out of sight at this time. I might not be taken for a teacher from the Pennock School." She looked at him with appraising eyes. "No more than you would be taken for a law wrangler."

"I guess you're right," he said, suddenly realizing they might have been dressed as twins were it not for the boots he preferred for long days in the saddle.

"Is that my horse?" Skye asked, nodding toward the tall, thickly-muscled sorrel that was saddled and tied behind Patch.

"Yes, unless you prefer the mare," Ethan said, pointing to the smaller, finer-boned gray that stood docilely behind the three pack horses.

Her dark eyes met his again, probing and evaluating, and made him slightly uneasy. "What is the horse's name?"

"Uh, Razorback."

She smiled, knowingly. Ethan could feel the heat of his embarrassment sliding down his neck. The woman moved up beside the big stallion, patted him softly on the neck and spoke to the wary animal in a low, soothing voice in what Ethan surmised was French. The stallion snorted challengingly and danced uneasily, but did not rear or strike.

Ethan suddenly had second thoughts about his prank. He did not want to hurt the young woman in spite of her arrogance and sharp tongue. The stallion was powerful and seemingly inexhaustible. And, he was ornery as hell. He'd broken the leg of more than one rider, fractured countless ribs in his career. He was a magnificent animal, but because of his disagreeable temperament, he had been retired to what Ethan thought was the enviable task of stud service at the Lazy R.

"Give me the reins," Skye said, still stroking the horse's neck and head.

Ethan untied the horse and handed her the reins. She took them in one hand, and, in a single fluid motion, without so much as touching the stirrup, grasped the horse's neck and lifted herself easily into the saddle. The stallion lurched forward as Skye settled into the saddle, throwing his hips sharply into Patch's flank as he brushed by. Momentary panic seized Ethan, as the horse raced away, but before he could nudge Patch to pursuit, Razorback slowed, whirled, and Skye dePaul, firmly in control, galloped back toward Ethan.

"He is a fine horse, Mr. Ramsey. Big and strong . . . and spirited," she said with a twinkle in her eyes.

"Yes, he is," Ethan agreed, adding grudgingly, "You obviously know how to handle horses, Miss dePaul."

Her face seemed to soften at his compliment. "Thank you, Mr. Ramsey. I could ride before I could walk."

"Would you mind calling me Ethan?" he asked her. "Mr. Ramsey makes me feel like an old man."

A glint of suspicion crossed her eyes briefly before she replied, "All right, Ethan," she said, "and you may call me Skye."

"That's an unusual name. I've never heard it before."

"It is something of an adaptation of my Sioux name, 'Sky-in-the-Morning.' That is how I am known to my mother. My father had my name recorded as Skye dePaul in his family Bible in deference to my mother. It was a way of showing his respect for her. He never thought of her as a squaw. To him, she was a woman and a wife whom he loved and treated as an equal."

"Why not?" Ethan asked.

Her face hardened again, and he had the feeling she had closed a window through which she had inadvertently let him see for just a moment.

"I think, Mr. . . . Ethan, we had better be on our way. I am not paying you for conversation. I presume you will attend to the supplies."

She kicked Razorback gently in the ribs, and the big horse lurched away.

5

THE TWO SAT cross-legged by the fire, facing each other across the orange-red glow of the flickering flames. They ate silently, devouring with animal-like enthusiasm the tough beef jerky and the sourdough bread Skye had baked on sticks while Ethan had staked out the horses.

Ethan watched Skye furtively as she attacked her simple meal. Somewhere along the way, as their little caravan had slowly climbed higher into the depths of the Rockies, Skye dePaul, French Quaker, was abandoned and Sky-in-the-Morning, Sioux maiden, took over. She was at home in this wilderness, at ease and comfortable, as much a part of the mountains as any deer or elk that roamed there.

Their trek up the winding, rocky trail that followed the rippling mountain stream that skirted their campsite had been a difficult one. The late afternoon sun had first squeezed the perspiration from their bodies, soaking their clothes with sweat and baked their skins dry so that he now felt like his body was encased in a curing animal hide. The sun had continued its work on the wrapped bodies anchored on the backs of the pack horses that followed grudgingly on the trail. The stench of death seemed to be everywhere and the horses, made skittish by it, had become increasingly stubborn and hard to handle as the day wore on.

Skye had controlled the horses with an authority he envied, and she had done more than her share of the work without complaint. They had not stopped until well after nightfall, and he was bone-weary, but he knew also that he would not get much sleep this first night on the trail. There was an adjustment his body always had to make before it accepted the old ways—hard ground, open sky, long days in the saddle, the tension wrought of ever-present danger.

Skye did not show any outward sign of stress, but she probably would not confess to discomfort in any case. They had spoken little since their departure from the bridge rendezvous. No casual conversation had passed between them. Surprisingly, they had communicated well without speaking—a simple nod when it was time for a pause on the trail, a gesture with the hand to warn that loose rock might be a hazard. And where before they had been inclined to argue and confront, they now worked compatibly in silence, each compensating instinctively for the other when problems arose on the trail.

They had not conferred about their campsite, but almost simultaneously—and he truly could not say who had made the first move—they had dismounted on the trail and led the horses some hundred feet over a twisting path that weaved through the dense growth of aspen and into the cozy, grassy clearing where they now camped. It was an idyllic setting with the soft hum of the mountain stream rushing over the rocks and mourning doves cooing and owls hooting softly in the background. A gentle evening breeze rustled the leaves of the whispering aspen that fringed the camp perimeter. So peaceful and restful. It was difficult to remember that terror and death could descend upon such a place so quickly. But civilization had not yet arrived in this part of Wyoming. In ten years, or a little more, a man would be able to bring his son to these mountains for a camping and hunting trip—but not now.

"If we start early tomorrow, can we make it to your uncle's village before nightfall? The bodies," he nodded toward the two stiff heaps resting side by side in the grass at the far end of the clearing, "they're pretty bad."

"No," she replied "I think not. The last stretch of the trail to the summer encampment is very treacherous, quite narrow, and the outer edge drops off into a canyon that appears bottomless. No, I am sorry, but we will not want to try it at night. Lame Buffalo chose such a location for obvious reasons. It is very easy to protect, and the valley where the camp is located is rich in game and water."

"I guess we'll have to do the best we can then, but we're going to leave a trail of turkey buzzards a mile long tomorrow. They were gliding in plenty close today. I don't like the damned things."

"Oh, but that is Waconda, the Great Spirit's way of keeping our good earth clean. The vultures remove the carrion, the stinking flesh, and make our air breathe again. The scavengers perform a great service."

"Waconda. The Great Spirit. I thought you were a Quaker."

"Not here."

"I thought as much. Your religion is not something of great conviction then?"

She was quiet a moment. "Perhaps you could say that. I think of myself as very religious. I believe there is some spiritual force that we cannot begin to comprehend that created this world." She lifted her hands in an open gesture to the sky, "One that made all of this possible. But I think we are essentially responsible for our own lives and what we do with them. Much religion, Sioux and white, is founded upon superstition, convenience and wishful thinking."

"Yet away from these mountains, you wear the Quaker garb. Doesn't that seem hypocritical?"

She did not seem miffed by his suggestion. "Probably. Are not most of us hypocritical at one time or another? In my own case, I was educated from childhood in a small Quaker school near Cheyenne. My father was Catholic, incidentally, although a rather casual one, but he felt that the Quakers would give me the best education to cope with the white man's world. They are a very good people, by and large, sincere in their beliefs, constructive influences in this country. I wanted to teach among my people. In this part of the West, Quakers provide almost the only outlet for teaching by someone of my blood. So, I embraced the Quaker religion, you might say, out of convenience. I try to abide by the rules when I live among them, though I must confess that my temper occasionally makes it difficult. I do not adhere very strictly to thee and thou pronouns like my sisters at the school."

"Do you plan to spend the rest of your life teaching?"

"I do not know. I enjoy it, but I do not see it as an end in itself. I will do something else when and if it suits me. I like to write. I have thought of writing. I enjoyed helping my father in his business. Sometimes the world of commerce intrigues me."

"You're a woman. Don't you ever think of a home?"

She smiled wryly. "Home? For the likes of me? There is no home for a halfbreed. Quakers accept me as a member of their religious family, but there is no true home for me among the whites. My mother never found one; that is why she returned to her people when my father died."

"And you have no home among the Brule?"

"Of course not. They are uncomfortable in my presence. I am welcome as a visitor. The men look upon me as something of a witch, I fear, tainted by a world they know little of. I respect my people; we have many intelligent, brave men and women among them. But can you imagine me as a squaw in the village of my people?"

"No, I guess not," he conceded.

"You have a home, do you not?"

"I do now. My ranch. I'll never leave it permanently. It's not much, but it's a place to return to, a place to sink my roots. It's my little piece of the world."

"But what if someone takes it away?"

"I won't let them."

"My people say that your 'piece of the world' once belonged to the Sioux, to all the tribes that roamed the plains and mountains of this part of what we now call Wyoming Territory. Their piece of the world is becoming smaller and smaller as each day passes. Soon they will have none."

"It's got to stop somewhere," he said. "I'm sympathetic, but I don't know the answer to how we reconcile the conflict between advancing civilization—that's what we call it anyway—and the way of life of your people."

"It will not stop," she said, "this thing your people call progress. It is inevitable, and some will be eaten up in the process.

Unfortunately, my people are the food for the cannibals. I do not like it, but we have to accept sometimes what we do not like or we shall cannibalize ourselves. My people must accept it and eventually adapt to the white man's ways if they are to survive as a race. It is that simple."

"Whites are your people, too," he reminded.

"True, I am not unmindful of that. I am proud of my white blood as I am of my Sioux, even though I feel it sometimes places my existence in no man's land. Perhaps it is the white in my blood that makes me want to help the Indians become a part of the white man's world, and it is the Sioux blood in me that makes me want to do it in a way that preserves the customs, culture and dignity of the Indian."

"I've never heard it put that way," Ethan said. "It's a nice thought. Altruistic, maybe, but a beautiful thought."

"Ethan, you said you had found a home, but you left much unsaid. Where was your home before?"

"I had none."

"What do you mean?"

"As near as I know, I was a bastard." He shivered involuntarily at the statement, realizing he had never told anyone before. "When I told you before I was half Swiss and half German, I was being sarcastic, I was raised in an orphanage in St. Louis. I didn't appreciate it at the time, but I received a good education there until I reached sixteen and the wanderlust hit me. It was rather traditional that boys at the orphanage run away at about that age. No roots, nothing to hold us there except a certain security for a few more years. Nobody cared by that time whether I stayed or went. I went. I caught on with a wagon train heading west. The wagon master hired me on as a general camp boy. No cash wages, just my meals and a wagon to sleep under."

"The train's scout took a liking to me; he was one of the best. He started teaching me the trade. We worked together for a few years until the Sioux finally lifted his scalp . . . Oglala, not Brule. Then I got a job scouting for the army. First, out of Fort Kearny in Nebraska, then Fort Laramie. I got to be Chief of Scouts at Laramie, not because of my superior scouting ability, but because I was the only one in the bunch who could read or write, and somebody had to write reports. I got the job and the title that went with it."

"It was more than that," she said. "I have heard stories from my people."

"Well, I don't mind being held in high esteem by your people, but the price of that could be my scalp." He noted she did not bother to deny it.

"What turned you to the law?"

"I'm an accidental lawyer. I observed that lawyers tended to be the trailblazers in establishing communities, setting up the structure and organization to make things work. A town without lawyers is a town without law. And a town without law is anarchy where nobody's person or property is secure. But beyond that, I was an opportunist."

"What do you mean by that?"

"There aren't many lawyers in the territory. Like I said before . . . I don't even know who my parents were. No home, no roots. I wanted a home and roots. I think most people do. Deep down, you do, too. I can tell as much about you by what you haven't said as by what you have. Anyway, I could see that by the time I was forty, there'd be no career as an army scout, and I'd end up swamping out bars someplace. I thought about it a lot. I had fallen in love with this country, and I wanted to stay here. I just had to find the best way to make a place for myself. I concluded there was something I could do that a lot of people out here couldn't—that was read and write. I always could write quite well. I thought back to the people I had heard about in St. Louis who were successful financially, those who were influential early in our country's history. Think about the men in the East who were the country's movers, the people who set the course. Hell, three-fourths of them were lawyers."

"That's true enough," Skye agreed.

"Lawyers are going to run Wyoming someday, too. And we're in cattle country here, so I thought law and cattle wouldn't be a bad deal. I purchased some law books and when my last tour of duty as an army scout was up, I approached my predecessor in Lockwood about reading law in his office. He was eager to leave, and saw a chance to sell out if he could get me through it. He left two weeks after I passed the bar."

"And you got in the cattle business?"

"When I knew I was going to stay in Lockwood, I took the small savings I had accumulated as an army scout and made a down payment on the ranch. My partner's an old army friend of mine." He smiled and shrugged. "That's the story of my life. I'm afraid my motives aren't quite as noble as yours. I want a home. I want roots. Along with that, I'd like to have influence and some money. I thought it might be nice to be Governor after statehood."

"Why not a United States Senator?" she asked teasingly.

"Very simple . . . I don't ever want to leave my mountains."

"If you are so guided by pragmatism, what are you doing here tonight? Why are you risking your life to take two dead Indian boys back to their Sioux village?"

"It's still pragmatism. You paid me a good retainer. I said I want to have money; I don't have it now. I'm flat broke and in debt up to my neck. Contrary to what some people think, and to what I once believed myself, lawyers don't get rich overnight. A lot of them die broke; plenty die drunkards. There's as much failure and unhappiness among members of the bar as anyplace else. Maybe more, because the expectations tend to be so much greater. No, I'm here for the money," he insisted.

"But helping the Sioux is not going to enhance your career."

"Oh, you never know how things might turn out. People aren't as narrow-minded as they used to be. But it still comes down to the fact that I need fees now; I'll worry about next year's mortgage payment next year."

"I do not think I have you figured out yet, Ethan."

"Nor I, you. But at least we're talking."

"Yes, at least we are talking. Ethan?" she said softly, her head unmoving, a flash of alarm in her eyes.

"I noticed. It's too quiet; birds have stopped calling."

"It has just been a few seconds," she said. "Whoever is coming is still down the trail, five, ten minutes away." She glanced back over her shoulder. "What do you think?"

He noticed her hand had clutched the bone handle of her skinning knife. "One of us has to stay as a decoy," he said, "until we find out who it is. If they see a woman here, they'll expect a man to be somewhere else. But not the other way around. Can you handle the Winchester you have wrapped in your bedroll?"

Her eyes turned to cold steel. "Trust me," she said simply.

"I'll have to." He reached for his own rifle and pulled it close, then slipped his Colt Peacemaker from its holster and spun the chamber into position before he re-holstered it. "You head for the trees then, and we'll wait it out, see what happens. I'll try to stay on this side of the fire, so consider anybody on the other side fair game if there's trouble."

Without a word, she snatched up her rifle and in a few moments disappeared into the darkness.

6

ETHAN WAITED IN front of the fire, his shoulders slouched, and his head slumped on his chest, as though enjoying an after-supper doze. He could hear footsteps on the path that led from the main trail to the campsite. There were two of them, but they weren't Indians. He would not have heard the Sioux.

"Hello, campers," came the thundering voice from just outside the clearing.

Ethan looked up; his head bobbed drowsily, feigning surprise. A big, beer-bellied man with a scraggly beard stepped into the clearing. The man raised his long arms above his head. "No harm intended, friend. I was on the trail and saw your fire. Thought there might be coffee and company here." The big man advanced, lowering his hands slowly as he moved closer. His eyes moved warily from side to side. "You alone, friend?"

"Yes," Ethan lied, knowing that the man could not have missed the two bedrolls spaced some five feet apart off to one side of the fire. Damn, he had been out of the business too long; it could cost him his life if he didn't watch out.

"You alone?" Ethan countered.

"Yep."

Ethan's own hand edged closer to his Peacemaker. Suddenly, the crack of a rifle exploded in the heavy night air. Reflexively, Ethan dove to his left, drawing his Peacemaker and rolling several times in the grass before he sprang up with the pistol leveled in the direction of his visitor. The big man, taken off guard by the gunshot behind him, drew his own pistol and fired off a hurried shot, and Ethan felt the searing pain at the base of his neck before he deliberately squeezed the trigger to put a bullet through the man's right eye. The man, gun still clutched in his hand, stumbled forward and collapsed in a heap in the ground.

Instinctively, Ethan's hand went to his right shoulder and grasped at the throbbing pain. Warm, slimy wetness there told him he was bleeding heavily. His body went weak.

He looked out into the darkness, his Peacemaker poised but shaky in his hand. "Skye," he called, "Skye?"

She came out from the trees, her rifle cradled in one arm. "Are you all right, Ethan?" she responded, looking at him quizzically. "I got the two back there."

"Two?" he asked before his knees buckled and blackness devoured him.

The darkness was still there when his eyes opened, but the stars that spangled the night sky told him he was alive. He started to lift himself up, but the vertigo hit him again, and he lay back, surrendering to it. He saw Skye moving toward him from the red hot coals of what remained of the fire.

"Would you take some coffee?" she asked. "The air is getting chilly and you need some fluid. You have lost a lot of blood."

"Yeah, I think so," he said, getting up on one elbow, suddenly conscious of the searing pain in his neck and shoulder.

Skye knelt down and pressed the cup to his lips. The shock of the steaming hot liquid in his mouth and throat brought him abruptly back to his senses. He accepted another drink and then lay back down.

"Thanks. Just leave the cup here. I'll be all right in a little while."

"I know you will," she said. "You are not hurt badly."

"I'm not? It hurts like hell." He touched his neck gingerly where Skye had made a compress of a shirt she had torn up and anchored by wrapping his chest and shoulder. "Did you get the bullet out?"

"There was none to remove. It looked more like a knife slice than a bullet wound. And as much as you bled, it should be a clean wound."

"The man . . . where—"

"I dragged him into the brush."

"How?"

"With a rope and Razorback pulling like a plow horse. I think Razorback was insulted. You will have to help bury him in the morning, though. A little scratch like you have will not get you out of that," she announced unsympathetically.

"Was I dreaming, or did I hear you say something about two other men before I went down? I only saw the big man. And I heard you take out another."

"You heard correctly, but there was one on the trail with their horses."

"What happened to him? I only heard one rifle shot."

"I cut his throat."

Ethan's brow furrowed in disbelief. "You what?"

"I cut his throat. It was the only way I could handle him quietly. If I had shot him, it would have warned the others. It was not very sporting of me, but I shot the second man in the back. He had his rifle aimed right at your chest. He did not appear very patient."

"Jesus," Ethan whispered.

"Do not worry; I did not scalp them," she said. "Not yet, anyway."

"You're not serious?"

She looked at him sober-faced, but the mischievous sparkle in her eyes betrayed her.

"Did you recognize any of the men?" he asked.

"No, but I think they were professional gunmen."

"What makes you say that?"

"When I left here, I went back to the trail and waited for them so I could follow them in. I could hear them talking. The big man, the one you shot, said something about Mr. Webb paying them the rest of the money when they brought back your scalp. They mentioned Webb's name several times."

"Gideon Webb? The rancher?"

"I did not hear a first name."

"I only know of two Webbs in the valley—Gideon and his son, Clete. I've never met Clete, just know him when I see him. And I've never had any trouble with Gideon Webb. He always seemed a decent sort of fellow. I've handled a few routine matters for him since I came to town. Property transactions. He was a congenial man. I had the feeling he was trying me out and I had hopes of a continuing relationship. A client like Circle W can make your bread and butter. To my knowledge, I've never done anything to alienate him. No reason to."

"Ethan," Skye scolded, "you are not naive. If the man wanted to have you killed before, he could have picked his time and place. But now? And here? It could have something to do with the attack on the Harper ranch."

He sighed and shook his head, trying to fight off the drowsiness that was overtaking him. "It doesn't add up."

"Is he land hungry?" she asked. "Does he want the Harper place?"

"Oh, he probably wants it all right. It lies next to the Circle W, but it's not especially strategic for water supplies or anything like that. But we ranchers are all alike, I suppose; we all want the land that lies next to us. Most of us are empire builders in a way, although my place barely qualifies as a ranch, let alone an empire. Still, you keep thinking how that neighbor's place would fit in with yours, what you could do to develop it. Then you see your place on the county map, taking up a little bit more of the county as each year goes by."

"That sounds like greed to me."

"Call it what you want, but that doesn't mean a man would kill for it. In fact, in my experience, I'd hold ranchers, as a group, pretty well above the rest of the population. In terms of honesty, their word is their bond, and while they're individualistic and aggressive, they're also high-principled. Sure, there are some bad ones, but I've never seen anything to indicate that Gideon Webb was one of them. Hell, my place would fit in better with the Circle W operation than Harper's. I can't imagine that Webb's mixed up in this thing, but it bears checking out. Something else bothers me more, though."

"What is that?" Skye asked.

"Well, half the town probably knew I'd hauled those boys out to my ranch on a buckboard, but for all they knew I was going to bury them. How many people knew I was going to Lame Buffalo's village and why I was going? If our friends out there were sent to stop us from getting to the village, then they had to know I planned to bring back Bear Killer and get to the bottom of the Harper killings."

"It does not take a lawyer to figure that out, Ethan."

"Skye, did you talk to anyone else about our plans?"

"No."

"How about Red Horse?"

"No. He knew we were taking the boys back to the village, but nothing else."

"He's Pawnee," Ethan said, "and they've been enemies of the Sioux for generations. Pawnee scouts fight Sioux for the pleasure of it."

"Not Red Horse. We are friends. He is like an old uncle to me, probably because of my Indian blood, and he has lived around the whites too many years. He is not interested in any blood feud. I would stake my life on it."

"You may be right. Let's look at my side of the ledger. Ben Dobbs knows what I'm up to; no problem there. The only other person is Katherine Wyeth."

"Your secretary?"

"Yes. I didn't give her any specifics, only that I would be gone for three or four days while we returned the Indian boys to their village. Of course, she knows that you retained my services. But she could have learned more."

"How?"

"By snooping through my personal notes in your file. After I confer with a client, I write out a fairly detailed memorandum of pertinent facts—the action I propose to take, that sort of thing. Katherine Wyeth would have access to those notes, and she could be especially nosey about this case."

"Because an Indian is involved?"

"Possibly. She didn't like you much."

"That was obvious."

"And I know she wasn't too keen on accepting someone with Indian blood as a client."

"But what good would the information do her even if she did have it? How would she know what to do with it?"

"I don't know. She's worked in law offices for a long time, so she should know the importance of keeping confidences. She could have talked out of turn, though, especially if she was upset. She's temperamental as hell. I don't think it was intentional; she wouldn't have a job if something happened to me. She won't have a job if I find out she had anything to do with this. I don't know," he mumbled, "I just don't know." His eyelids started to drift shut.

"Go to sleep, Ethan," Skye said as she pulled the blankets up over his shoulders. "You'll need all the rest you can get for tomorrow."

She got up and moved to her own bedroll which, before he finally surrendered to an exhausted sleep, Ethan noticed had been moved to within reach of his own.

7

BENEATH A THIN layer of rich humus, the mountain soil was dry and rocky, and Ethan had neither the strength nor the inclination to hollow out more than shallow, common graves for the three would-be assassins. The rock and shale, raked and piled over the dead men, would offer no more than token resistance to the predators that would soon descend upon the slope, but somehow the performance of the ritual salved Ethan's conscience and made him feel civilized.

Skye dePaul had the horses saddled and ready to ride, and by the time Ethan finished his job, all that remained was the additional unpleasant task of loading and tying the bodies of the Indian boys to the pack animals. Ethan nearly gagged at the stench that rose from the blanket-wrapped corpses as he and Skye finished hitching them to the pack horses.

"I see you've added our friends' horses to the string," Ethan remarked, nodding toward the horses at the rear.

"Yes," she said. "They will be gifts to Lame Buffalo. And their rifles, too. My uncle will be especially pleased to receive the rifles."

"Damn it, Skye. I don't know. Now you've got me gun-running, too. I think that's going a bit too far. The horses, well, I suppose that's all right, although their legal status is a little shaky. But the guns—"

"I am not asking you for your advice on either the horses or the guns, Mr. Attorney," she said coolly. "This is my mission. You are accompanying me only as my lawyer. I shall assume full responsibility for disposition of the spoils. Besides, how do you propose to keep my uncle from taking these things and everything else we have as well? Is it not better to tender them as gifts and secure his good will?"

She made sense, but ruffled by her abrupt manner, Ethan was not about to concede it. "Oh, hell, have it your way," he growled, as he moved for his horse. "As you say, I'm just a hired hand."

"I did not say that," she countered. "I said you are my lawyer. Please do not be so sensitive."

"Let's get moving," Ethan said. "We're apt to run into some of your kinsmen today, and they might shoot first and ask questions later. One of us had better stay toward the rear. Why don't you handle that . . . you can keep an eye on your 'spoils' that way."

Her eyes blazed and she opened her mouth as though to retort, but then turned quickly away, mounted Razorback, and nudged him to the rear of the caravan.

Skye dePaul had been right about one thing the night before: he had needed rest. He was exhausted and suspected he was suffering from dehydration. After he tied the last of the horses to the picket line, Ethan had collapsed in front of the towering ponderosa where he now sat. The day had been a grueling test of his endurance, the trail steeper and the footing more precarious than the day before. It had also been hotter and drier and windier. And the horses had been nervous and balky. And Skye had been more disagreeable. But in spite of the obstacles, they had made good time, reaching their destination by late afternoon.

The placid, mirror-like lake near which they now camped reflected the emerald spires of the ponderosa that cloaked the rocky slopes and provided an ample windbreak, and the thick, luxuriant grass along the lakeside provided abundant grazing for the horses. It was the last sanctuary before the final ascent that would lead them above the valley of Lame Buffalo's summer camp.

They were vulnerable to attack. He would never have led a cavalry patrol to this spot, for the surrounding ridges left them in a bowl, and they could be swallowed up in seconds by a sweep of attacking Sioux. But it no longer mattered. Any thought of safety now was an illusion because they were in the heart of the Brule.

"My people know we are here," Skye had said earlier. "You now live at their pleasure."

He had known that, but hearing her say it, and the way she had said it, had left him cold.

The fiery glow of the sun had crept behind the mountain peaks and dusk was rapidly settling on the glen. Skye had built a fire that was burning down to red-hot cooking embers now.

She had disappeared some time earlier, and he had resigned himself to fixing supper. The woman was not inclined to draw a clear line between male and female domain. Hell, it wasn't her Sioux blood that kept her a spinster. Any man who ran up against her would see that marriage would be a lifelong struggle over who got to wear the pants in the family. Of course, you could have two pair of pants, he supposed.

Her strength and independence attracted him, he admitted, and he was intrigued, stimulated, by her intelligence and the aura of mystery that surrounded her, a mystery that evolved from the unique way two cultures had come together in this woman, blending in some ways, yet clashing and irreconcilable in others.

He looked over at the smoldering fire and hunger pangs sliced through his belly. Oh, what the hell. He got up stiffly and decided he would start the coffee brewing and maybe grab some beef jerky to pacify his stomach. As he got up, the dull, throbbing pain commenced in his neck again. A bath, that's what he needed. A steaming, hot tub bath. But any bath would feel good now, just to wash away the dirt and grime, to ease the soreness in his neck.

The lake, fed by mountain springs and melting snow from the peaks above, would be ice cold, but it would cleanse and soothe, he knew, for he was not a stranger to mountain streams and lakes. He headed for the inviting water, deciding that coffee and supper could wait.

He peeled off his shirt when he reached the lake's edge, but stopped dead in his tracks at the sight of the brown-skinned nymph swooping and gliding in the water off the fingerlike projection of rock not more than a hundred feet down the lakeshore. He watched her, mesmerized by the grace and ease with which she moved in the water, like an otter, born to it, a part of it.

Momentarily, she emerged and lifted herself up on to the craggy rock. She did not see him. She stood there and brushed her wet black hair back over her shoulders and then faced the lake and opened her arms as if to catch the breeze that drifted off it. She was a statue, a young goddess, standing there against a backdrop of shimmering colors muted by the fading light. Her body muscular, yet sleek. Her breasts small, but well defined. Her face uplifted, almost posed. The embodiment of an artist's vision. His heart hammered and his pulse quickened; desire surged through him. How long since he had had a woman? The saloon girl in Cheyenne? Three months? Now it seemed like three years.

Suddenly, as if she had felt the heat of his gaze, she turned and faced him. She stood there naked, unashamed, and he was glad that he could not see her eyes, for in that instant he felt lower than a peeping tom.

Then, without particular haste, she bent over and picked up her clothing and began to dress. Ethan did not move, embarrassed by the unabashed scrutiny he had given her, yet uncertain after having been caught in the hen house, what protocol demanded.

She approached him quietly, and he saw she carried a string of lake trout in her hand. Her face was stern, mildly reproachful, but he saw no anger there.

"I will prepare these for supper," she said softly.

"Skye, I—"

She turned away and hurried up the path, for which he was grateful because he had not the slightest idea what he would have said. He walked to the lakeside, finished disrobing and waded out into the water. Shivers raced down his spine and goosebumps broke out on his skin as the water and its icy coldness consumed him. The stiffness in his shoulder would not permit him to swim, but once he adapted to the frigidity of the water, he soaked and bathed and was invigorated by it. He stayed longer than necessary, and when he got out he discovered that the air had turned chilly, almost biting. Nonetheless, he stood there, letting the dry mountain air sponge out the water from his skin before he dressed.

As he started to slip into his buckskin shirt, he saw that a tiny stream of scarlet was working its way down his chest, and realized that the water had softened the scab on the wound and reopened it.

"Come back to camp," Skye's voice came from up the slope. "I will redress your wound."

He could not see her in the darkness, hidden by the shadowy veil of ponderosa, but with the reflection of the full moon glow off the quiet water, he knew he might as well have been standing in the center of a brightly-lit room. How long had she been standing there? Long enough.

This night there was no talking by the campfire. Skye silently re-bandaged Ethan's wound with hands that seemed unnecessarily rough and harsh, but he apologized to her mentally when she served the banquet of roasted trout, hot black coffee, and the traditional sourdough bread.

"Delicious," he commented, breaking the silence between them.

"You may prepare breakfast. You will not be pampered after tonight."

"Yes, ma'am," he replied meekly.

Drowsiness overtook him early again, reminding him that he had not yet recovered his strength. The cool night air had turned downright cold, and he was ready to burrow into his bedroll for refuge. "Damn, it's cold," he remarked as he stood up. "I'm going to move my bedroll next to the fire and turn in."

"You have a fever," she said. "I noticed when I dressed your wound. I think it is nothing serious; the wound does not seem to be festering."

He spread out his bedroll next to the fire; then as he crawled into the cocoon of blankets, he saw that Skye was laying her own bedroll out next to his. He looked at her quizzically, hopefully, but his hopes were quickly dampened.

"Our blankets will remain between us," she said, "but you will be warmer if I sleep here."

She was right. The woman on one side made him warmer than the fire on the other. Nonetheless, sleep eluded him only briefly, and soon, he surrendered to death-like slumber.

8

Skye shook Ethan awake the next morning. His eyes opened and then scrunched nearly shut as they were blinded by the early morning sunshine.

"Ethan," Skye whispered, "we will have visitors soon. I think they are warriors from Lame Buffalo's encampment. There are five or six of them from the sound. They are coming up the trail. It is probably a hunting party."

"Or a war party," he said glumly as he got up.

"No, I think not. Not this soon."

"Shall I fix breakfast?" he asked. "Maybe some bacon and biscuits for our guests? We have plenty." He got up and commenced rummaging through the supplies. Skye moved to help him.

"You do not seem greatly disturbed," she said.

"I'm scared as hell," he growled, "but right now, my fate is in hands of God, or the Great Spirit or whatever else you want to call Him. All I can do is give Him a little help."

Skye tensed and her eyes fixed on something behind Ethan. "What is it?" he asked, knowing the answer to his own question.

Ron Schwab

"They are here. On the ridge, behind you."

Ethan turned slowly and looked toward the rise from where the five mounted warriors surveyed the camp. "Should we call them in?" Ethan asked.

"Yes, I think so. Do you speak our language?"

"Some, but I'm not fluent. I think it's best if I play dumb for now. You do the talking."

"Very well." She lifted her hand in greeting, and in Brule dialect invited the warriors to enter the camp. They rode their horses single file, slowly and cautiously, down the shale-covered slope. As they rode closer, Skye said, "I know several of them. The front warrior, the small one, he will be the spokesman. He is called Badger Claw. He is a fine warrior . . . and a cunning fox. When I was but a girl, he asked my uncle if I might be his second wife. It is said that a mighty weapon lies under his breechcloth."

He caught a trace of an impish smile on her lips, and it made her face seem warmer and less severe. From their first meeting, she had been so businesslike, almost cold-blooded, that now the change in her demeanor puzzled him.

"Do not worry, Ethan," she said. "We will get to the village. Badger Claw controls these men . . . and I can control Badger Claw."

The Indians rode into the camp, their unpainted faces stoic, their eyes wary. Several had feathers knotted in their hair. Three wore buckskin leggings and one, a stiff, soiled war shirt.

But Badger Claw was naked except for the narrow loincloth that girded his loins and the moccasins that covered his feet. In spite of the Sioux's small stature, Ethan could see from the sinewy muscles that sheathed his frame that the man would be a superb athlete. The body would be quick and finely coordinated. The Indian, probably approaching forty, was handsome by any standards—hair braided neatly and his bronze skin clean and glistening in contrast to the dirty, greasy appearances of his comrades who showed effects of a long absence from the village. This warrior Indian was a peacock, but he flaunted his body instead of his feathers.

Strangely, Ethan felt a pang of envy when he saw Skye's eyes surveying the obvious leader of the hunting party. Badger Claw's eyes locked on the wrapped bodies that had been left some distance downwind from the camp. "You have come to visit Lame Buffalo?" the warrior asked in Sioux. "We have not seen you in our village for many moons."

"I am returning the bodies of two brave boys to their people," Skye responded in her native language. "This man helps me."

"And how did these boys come to die?"

"My cousin Bear Killer was there. My uncle knows," Skye said. "It is his place to say."

Skye was trading heavily on her relationship to the Chief. Ethan could see that the warrior was miffed by her evasiveness, but that he was hesitant to do anything that might invoke the wrath of the Chief. Badger Claw studied Skye appraisingly.

She met his gaze evenly. The warrior edged his pony closer to Ethan, glaring at the white man, his eyes seething with hate. This would have been the end of the journey if he had come alone, Ethan thought.

"Do you know this man, Sky-in-the-Morning?" the Indian asked, without taking his eyes off Ethan.

"Of course," she said nonchalantly, "I have traveled with him." She added meaningfully, "For two days and two nights. He is a good friend—an honorable and brave man. His name is Ethan Ramsey."

"He is the Puma," the Indian said. "He is an enemy. I have fought him."

"He is no longer an enemy. We are at peace. This man no longer rides with the pony soldiers."

"Then he is a coward," Badger Claw declared.

"He is a friend and under the protection of your Chief," Skye lied. "We leave for Elk Valley this morning, but first we must eat. You are invited to join us."

Badger Claw turned and nodded to his companions. They dismounted and tied the ponies at the edge of the clearing.

Ethan turned to the supplies. "Pompous little bastard," he grumbled. "Too bad we don't have some rat poison."

"Ethan, sit down," Skye commanded. "I will fix breakfast."

"I'll do it . . . I'll help anyway."

"No," she said, "just add another meal to your debt. They know who you are. A great warrior does not do women's work. They do not like you, but they respect you . . . and we may need the respect later on."

"I'm glad you're finally acknowledging that something is women's work," he said.

"I am not acknowledging anything. I am telling you how the Sioux look upon it. That is one reason I cannot live permanently in their world."

"Hell, I don't see what difference it makes. You'd have everything changed a year after you moved into the village anyway."

"I think you would do well to get along with me," she cautioned as she commenced slicing a slab of smoked bacon.

9

THEIR DESCENT DOWN the narrow mountain trail that led into Elk Valley was a silent, sober one. Badger Claw headed up the caravan while the other warriors followed Skye dePaul and Ethan, who led the pack animals. Their approach through the lush meadow that surrounded the Sioux encampment did not go unnoticed, and by the time they broke through the perimeter of tepees, some of the squaws, guessing the contents of the shrouded bundles, burst into eerie wailing and chanting, and fell in beside the horses as they continued slowly toward Lame Buffalo's tepee at the far end of the village.

The busy, ant-like activity of the camp came to an abrupt halt. Sullen-faced braves and warriors watched the procession as it weaved through the village. The children, who had been absorbed in play, scurried out of the riders' path.

Skye had been silent and thoughtful throughout the journey and offered him no encouragement. "It will be difficult," she declared solemnly in a soft voice. For the first time since he met her, Skye's demeanor seemed something less than confident.

Moments later, as they sat cross-legged before Lame Buffalo

in the Chief's lodge, a demure, almost shy side of the woman emerged. She sat solemnly beside Ethan, her head bowed slightly before Lame Buffalo's scrutiny. Ethan knew it would be disrespectful of him to speak first, and he suspected that Skye was accepting her own subservient status as a woman in the village and would not break the silence.

The grim-faced Badger Claw, hate burning in his obsidian eyes, sat to the right of the Chief, confirming that he was a man of some import in the tribe, perhaps a sub-chief.

To the Chief's left sat an ancient, white-haired man, his body squat and fat, his jowly, stoic face dominated by porcine eyes that disclosed nothing. The elderly Sioux was clad in buckskin and the strips of beadwork that adorned his shirt indicated he, too, was a person of some rank, probably a medicine man. A man of such heft was a rarity among the plains Indians, and such a man, even in his prime, could not have been a war chief of the Brule Sioux.

Lame Buffalo carried himself with a bearing appropriate to his status. As the older Indian was unusually rotund for one of these people, so was Lame Buffalo exceptionally tall, and Ethan could see that Skye's own unusual height would have come from her uncle's side of the family. From what Skye had said, he surmised the Chief was in his late forties, but his powerful chest and shoulders were those of a man much younger. Most Indians he had known aged before their time. Lame Buffalo was a handsome man by any standard, his aquiline nose suited to the angular features of his unblemished face. He wore leggings with his breech cloth, but his torso was naked and absent any accoutrements of rank. But beyond this, and except for the slight limp from which Ethan assumed the man had derived his name, the Chief was a dime novel's stereotype of all that a chief should be.

Finally, the Chief spoke in Brule dialect, his eyes locked upon Skye, seemingly indifferent to Ethan's presence in the tepee. "Sky-in-the-Morning returns to her people bearing sad gifts," the Chief said. Skye looked up but did not reply. "My niece still refuses to behave as a squaw," the Chief added, with a faint tone of reprimand in his voice. But was that a glint of pride Ethan caught in Lame Buffalo's eyes?

"I am sorry, my uncle," Skye replied in Sioux. "But the way of the Brule is not my way."

"Then why have you returned the murdered youths? Why did you not leave them to rot in the village of the white man?"

Skye seemed less reticent now, her instincts, Ethan thought, beginning to overpower her desire to show respect for her uncle and his people.

"Because I do not accept the ways of my people, does not mean I cannot love my people," Skye replied, "or respect and honor their ways. My father was white and I have spent most of my life in the white world. I am Sky-in-the-Morning, not my mother, Singing Lark. I am the offspring of two worlds, neither of which I revere more than the other. But the great Sioux nation will someday be consumed by the white world. If the Great Spirit wills that I someday bear children, those children shall be raised in a white world as shall your grandchildren, my uncle, and great-grandchildren thereafter. I say this sadly, but it is true; therefore, I have chosen to accept that world and make my place in it."

The Chief nodded his head slowly, suddenly changing languages and speaking near-perfect English. "I understand, Sky-in-the-Morning, daughter of my sister. What you say is true. I feel it in my heart. But I cannot accept it. Not yet. And neither will my people." He was silent a moment. "You say that you will follow the ways of the white world. Will the white world accept you?"

"I shall make the white world accept me, my uncle," Skye replied.

Traces of a smile crossed the Chief's lips but quickly faded. He turned to Ethan, "In our village, she is still a squaw," he said. "If there is something to be said, it is better that you speak. Do you speak our tongue?"

"Yes," Ethan said, "some. But not nearly so well as you speak ours."

"Sky-in-the-Morning is a teacher in this place she calls the white man's world. She is also a teacher in her own village. She has taught me and many others your language. We shall use the tongue of the English between us. Badger Claw and Lone Elk will understand little of what we say; perhaps that is well." The Chief paused. "You are the one called the Puma, so I am told. You are a respected enemy of our people. You are very brave to come to our camp . . . or very stupid."

"Probably the latter," Ethan said sardonically, "but I do not think of myself as an enemy of your people. We are at peace now, and I no longer ride with the soldiers. Like your own warriors, I was a warrior fighting for my own people. I admire the Sioux, and I am not proud of much that my government has done to your people."

"Have you lain with Sky-in-the-Morning?" the Chief asked.

"No," he replied, meeting the Chief's gaze evenly. "Of course not. I am her lawyer, not her man."

"Lawyer?"

"Yes. Among my people are those who are paid to speak for others. They are called lawyers."

"Why do your people not speak for themselves?"

"Because we have a set of laws, written rules, by which our people must live. These rules are sometimes very complicated, hard for people to understand. A lawyer is trained to understand them and to help others understand them. We have judges who settle disputes over those rules and decide if people have broken them and how they should be punished if they did."

"Yes, I have heard of these judges, but I cannot see their purpose. I am the judge in our village. We need no written laws here, for our rules are simple and they have been passed from father to son for more winters than man can count. A man speaks for himself. We have no need for lawyers. I think that is good."

"It may be," Ethan said, "I sometimes wonder myself."

"But you have not lain with Sky-in-the-Morning? You do not like her?"

The Chief had a one-track mind. "Yes, I like her. She is—" He glanced at Skye, whose laughing eyes could not hide her amusement at his discomfiture. "She is a stubborn, contrary woman, on occasion not unlike the jackass. But I try not to hold that against her. Anyway, what I think of her is not important. I am not her man, but her lawyer, her spokesman among the white eyes. Besides, one who would seek to lie with Sky-in-the-Morning without first being her man would end up dead, I think."

Lame Buffalo nodded his head in understanding. "You are a wise man. I do not like this thing you call a lawyer. Sky-in-the-

Morning can speak for herself. But it is not proper that she speak here, so I will listen to you. Tell me, why are you here?"

Ethan related the story of his first meeting with Skye, and appreciating the Indians' susceptibility to superstition, mentioned the coincidence of the coyote's howling and Skye's inspiration to contact him. He affirmed his own belief in the Indian boys' innocence in no uncertain terms, and then told the Chief about the attack on the first night of their journey into the mountains. "I am convinced these things are related," he said, "but it must be proven. We think that your son, Bear Killer, should return with us to Lockwood so that he can tell our sheriff what he knows or does not know. Our sheriff is a good man. It is possible that Bear Killer would not even be charged with a crime. If he should be, I would be his lawyer and represent him before the judge and jury."

"Jury?"

"Yes, a jury is a group of citizens who decide whether one is innocent or guilty, and the judge decides the punishment based upon the law."

"This jury . . . they would be men from Lockwood?"

"Yes, and from some of the surrounding farms and ranches."

"And would this jury be fair? Would it say that an Indian is innocent?"

Ethan paused. "I cannot say that, Chief Lame Buffalo. If we can discover proof that someone else did it, then yes, I am confident the jury would find your son innocent. But many of these men have fought your people, lost wives and children in the Indian wars. I cannot promise how they would decide if we do not provide definite proof of Bear Killer's innocence. The burden of proof is supposed to work the other way, but it is not always so."

"You ask me to put my son to death. Do you think I am a fool?"

"No. That is why we are here. If this is not settled in the white man's court, there will be more wars. Already, the people of Lockwood are angry. Most will do nothing, but there are some who are looking for an excuse to kill. And this is the problem. They will find some of your people and kill them. Then your warriors will seek vengeance and kill whites. Then there will be more killing . . . and more. Many white men and Sioux, perhaps including your own son, will die in such a war. Blood will paint these mountains. We must stop it if it is within our power to do so, and I think it is."

"There are already those among my people who are impatient to take scalps." The Chief shot a meaningful look at Badger Claw. "They say that I, like Spotted Tail, have become an old woman. If I let you take my son and he does not return alive, they will not be stopped. I must lead them into battle, or they will choose another Chief. If my son should die, I will gladly lead them. It will not be these mountains, but the village of the white eyes that will be covered red with blood. You yourself have said my son did not do this thing. My people know this is true. I do not see why I should deliver him to this white man's jury. Why should I trust you with the life of my son?"

"You know the wisdom of my words, Lame Buffalo. You are a Chief because you see your people as tribe . . . a people. You know that the life of one cannot be permitted to jeopardize the existence of an entire nation, even when that one is your own child. That is the difference between a chief and a warrior."

The Chief's face was grave and Ethan could see he had

struck a responsive chord. "I'll give you this pledge, Lame Buffalo. . . . If your son returns to Lockwood with me, I will protect him with my own life. I will not let him be put to death under white man's law. . . . I promise that."

"I do not trust the white man's law. How am I to know you do not speak with forked tongue?"

"Because I have never lied to your people, and because I know I am a dead man if I betray the Sioux."

"If I heed the words of Badger Claw, you are a dead man anyway. He would like your scalp to decorate his war lance."

"I am not worried. Badger Claw is not the Chief of this village. Lame Buffalo is said to be a man of honor; I have come in friendship, and I have brought no harm to your people. I know you do not like this idea of a lawyer, but your people need a lawyer in the village of my people."

"I will think on this," said the Chief. "You will know what I decide when the sun rises. You will leave then. Maybe alone."

10

THE HAIR BRISTLED on the back of Ethan's neck, and a shiver danced down his spine. It was nothing he could put a finger on, just the same instinct that had made him a good scout, the sixth sense that he had long since learned to trust unquestionably. Something was not right at the ranch.

The gray haze of dusk had settled on the valley, and all he could make out was the shadowy outline of the barn and corral against the fiery orange horizon. His view of the ranch house was obscured by the dense growth of mountain ash and ponderosa that sheltered the approach to the ranch buildings, and he was unable to detect any activity near the house. He reined in the Appaloosa and raised his hand to signal a halt to the two riders lagging behind with the pack horses.

"What is it, Ethan?" Skye asked as she sidled Razorback up beside him, leaving the sober-faced Indian boy with the pack animals.

Patch whinnied nervously and jerked his head sharply against the reins. "I don't know," Ethan said. "Patch is skittish as the devil, and it's awfully quiet down there." He slipped his

Ron Schwab

Winchester from the saddle holster, dismounted and handed Skye his horse's reins. "You and Bear Killer wait here. I think I'll walk on down and take a look."

"Do you want me to follow and cover you?"

He started to protest, but then thought better of it. If she had been a man, he would not have hesitated. It was just good sense to have someone backing you in a situation like this, and he already knew Skye dePaul could handle a gun. "Yes, it might be a good idea," he said.

Ethan headed down the slope while Skye led their horses back up the trail to Bear Killer and followed him a respectful distance. Ethan wound his way through the trees that provided a natural windbreak for the weathered, frame house and outbuildings. When he reached the edge of the clearing he stopped and looked out onto the ranch yard. It was still, deathly so. The corral gates were open, and the horses had been turned out. Ben had been trying to break some of the wild ones in the north corral and would not have turned them loose. Ethan glanced over his shoulder and saw that Skye waited further up the slope, her rifle readied in her hands.

He stepped cautiously into the open, his eyes scanning the building and corrals as he walked slowly across the ranch yard. Suddenly, the all-too familiar stench of rancid flesh seared his nostrils. It was human carrion he smelled; there was no other scent like it.

He angled into the breeze that wafted in from the foothills to the north, the increasing odor telling him as he moved to the far end of the yard that he was walking in the right direction.

Momentarily, he came upon what was left of Ben Dobbs. The corpse was a far cry from the Ben Dobbs Ethan remembered. Ben had been scalped, but someone had done a messy job of it and removed a fair chunk of his skull in the process. The body was bloated and Ben's face was grotesquely mutilated where the buzzards had been feasting and even shredded his shirt and trousers in the course of ravaging his remains. One more day and Ben Dobbs would have been picked to the bone.

Ethan moved closer, nudging the corpse with the barrel of his rifle. He had seen worse, but it was a struggle to keep from retching, for this particular body had housed his friend. That made a hell of a difference, Ethan thought. Death was never pleasant, but a dead stranger often seemed little more than a dead animal. The death of a friend or comrade always hit home. And Ben Dobbs was about as close as he had had in the way of family.

Ethan pushed away some of the ragged buckskin that covered Ben's chest and found the gaping hole that must have killed him. He guessed it was an old Sharps or other powerful rifle from the size of the wound. The bushwhacker must have caught Ben by surprise, for his six-gun was still holstered and his rifle was nowhere in sight. It didn't make sense. Ben's killer couldn't have moved in too close, or the old Indian fighter would have felt his presence. It would have taken a skilled marksman to nail Ben Dobbs. That pretty well ruled out most of the Sioux, but Ethan had not been fooled by the clumsy attempt to put the blame on the Indians in the first place.

"Ethan! Watch out!" came Skye's voice from behind.

Reflexively, he hit the ground and rolled, just as a rifle cracked and a bullet thudded into the earth where he had been standing. He heard Skye's rifle snap off two quick shots.

Someone groaned, and Ethan looked up to see a man at the north corner of the corral double up and slump to the ground as if he had been kicked in the groin. Then he heard hoofbeats as a horse, presumably that of an accomplice, raced away from the ranch.

He got up and dusted off his trousers and then looked back at Skye who stood with rifle poised at the corner of the house, her face expressionless, her dark eyes cold as steel. He waved acknowledgement.

"Thanks," he said. "Damn," he muttered under his breath as he strode toward the fallen, would-be killer. Skye dePaul might be half-white, but so far he had not seen much of the white half. She was full-blooded Sioux right now for damn sure.

Ethan knelt down and flipped the ambusher's body over on his back. The man was stone dead. Either bullet could have killed him. His chest was a sunburst of scarlet where one bullet had struck, but the bullet that had driven into his temple had probably killed him instantly.

Skye came up behind him. "Do you know the man?" she asked.

"No, I've never seen him before, but he's a gunslinger, not a cowboy."

"How do you know?"

Ethan gazed impassively at the contorted face of the lean, dark-haired man who lay sprawled in the dust. "His face, for one thing. Look how pale it is. A cowboy's skin would be brown and windburned this time of year. This guy lived in saloons except when his work took him outside. And the callous on his trigger finger on the right hand; he used a gun every day in regular practice sessions. Like a professional violinist. He carried his handgun low on the hip, and the rifle and pistol weren't cared for by a man who just respects his weapon; they were looked after by somebody who worshipped them. No, he was a professional. I'm damn lucky it isn't me lying there."

"But why?" Skye asked. "Why is this happening? Why your friend? That is your friend over there, is it not?" she asked, waving her rifle in the direction of Ben Dobbs's body.

"Yes, that's Ben . . . and I don't know why. But it's got to be for the same reason those birds tried to ambush us in the mountains. It's a good bet those men and this fellow had the same boss. It must have something to do with the murder of the Harpers and the hanging of the Sioux boys. My guess is that Ben Dobbs was on his way to getting it figured out, and that's why he's dead."

"Then perhaps Red Horse knows something," Skye said. "Maybe they found something at the Harper ranch. I could ride out to the Pennock School and talk to him."

"Not tonight," Ethan said. "If Red Horse knows anything important, he's probably already dead. Ben's been dead the better part of a two days. If they haven't got Red Horse by now, he'll still be at the Pennock School in the morning. Why don't you get back up the trail and bring Bear Killer and the horses in? I'll get a shovel and see to burying Ben. This hombre, I'll load into the Sheriff in the morning, then check at my office and take a ride out to the Pennock School."

"Are you going to take Bear Killer in?"

"No, not now. I want to be certain Sheriff Bridges is back. I think you and Bear Killer should stay at my place. At this point, I don't know who to trust, and I promised Lame Buffalo that Bear Killer would be safe in Lockwood. We can protect him here as well as any place right now. I'll send him back to your uncle's village before I turn him over to the law for slaughter."

Skye's eyes softened. "Thank you, Ethan," she said. "I think I selected a good lawyer for myself." Her face flushed slightly before she turned and walked away.

"Well, I'll be damned," Ethan whispered. "I think she just said something nice to me."

11

"CARTIN' AROUND CORPSES is gettin' to be kind of a habit with you, ain't it, Ethan?" Enos Fletcher chortled as Ethan dismounted in front of the livery stable. Enos scratched at his beard and studied the body that was slung over the back of the second horse.

"Do you know him?" Ethan asked.

"Sort of," the old man replied.

"What do you mean 'sort of'?"

"Him and another fellar rode in a couple of days ago. Put their horses up here the first night. Figured them for hired guns. Real dandies, both of them. Looks like I had 'em pegged; they was hired guns, wasn't they?"

"Yeah, Enos, I think that's a fair statement."

"Did you kill that jasper?"

"No."

"Did Ben do him in?"

"Ben's dead."

The old man frowned. "The hell you say. Goddamn. I'm right sorry, Ethan. Ben was a good man. . . . A hell of a good man. Did

Ron Schwab

this skunk kill him?"

"I don't know, Enos. I don't know who killed Ben . . . but I intend to find out,"

"Who did you say done this bird in?"

"I didn't. Let's just say it was a friend of mine."

Enos cocked his head to one side and looked at Ethan quizzically. "You sure don't talk much for a law wrangler, do you Ethan?"

"Sometimes a lawyer does his best work when he keeps his mouth shut. Tell me something, Enos. You say this guy rode in with another man. . . . What did he look like?"

"Younger by ten years. Barely twenty, I'd guess. Tall, skinny fellar with slick black hair. I'd guess he has a touch of Mex in him. Dark skin, thought he was hot shit. Had one of them smiles that wriggles the gals right out of their bloomers. Know the kind?"

"Yeah, I've got the picture."

"He carried one of them fancy pearl-handled revolvers, too. Shiny, black boots. Showboat type. But this here fellar, he was the boss man. The kid didn't give him no guff."

"Do you remember their names?"

"Not this one. The kid's name was Race. Race something, that's what this fellar called him. Race, now ain't that some name for a kid?"

"Different," Ethan agreed. "Can you tell me anything else?"

"Nope. Just saw them twice—once when they left the horses; once when they picked 'em up. Twice too many as far as I'm concerned."

"All right, Enos. Do me a favor, will you? Keep your ears open; let me know if you hear any more about those two. . . .

Anybody they talked to or did business with while they were in town."

"Maybe I will and maybe I won't," Enos said noncommittally.

"What do you mean?"

"Sometimes it ain't such a bad idea to keep your damn mouth shut in the livery business either."

"I guess you got me there, Enos," Ethan said. Then handing him Patch's reins, continued, "Take care of my horses, will you? I'll be back around noon."

"Sure, the horses I can handle. What about this hunk of dead meat? He's startin' to putrefy; I can't have him around here. Bad for business. Scares the hell out of the horses, too."

"Just drop him in the shade someplace. I'm going down to talk to Will. He'll probably want to take a look at him before the undertaker goes to work."

"George don't like county funerals; he ain't gonna be happy. He'll bellyache like hell."

"But the guy's white," Ethan reminded. "George will take care of him. If I know George, he'll find a way to screw the county."

Enos cackled, displaying his yellow fangs in a rare smile. "Damn you, Ethan, maybe you're smarter than you look. Lots of folks have been here ten years and ain't never caught on to George. Good old God-fearing George, they say. Shit," Enos spat a stream of gooey tobacco on the ground at Ethan's feet. "Double shit. If folks knew what I knew about old George. Hell, he comes in here his pecker so hard he can hardly sit down. Runs out to the widow Brown's every Wednesday and Saturday just like clockwork. If his old lady knew what kind of evangelism work he was doing for the Methodists, she'd run his balls through a coffee grinder. I can tell you something else about old George, too, you know," said Enos.

"Some other time, Enos. I'm late and I've got a lot to get done this morning. I'll see you later. And about our friend and his partner, Race . . . well, I've got a client who might pay pretty well for some bits of information. Just keep that in mind, will you?"

A greedy glint surfaced in the livery man's eyes. "Like I say, Ethan, sometimes it pays in my business to talk a lot."

As Ethan stepped onto the boardwalk that edged Lockwood's main street, he glanced back over his shoulder and noticed a little cluster of old men and small boys was beginning to congregate at the livery stable. Enos had an audience, so he wouldn't be putting up the horses for a spell. God knows what kind of tale Enos would spin. But at least word would be out. The undertaker had a new customer, and the right persons would find out before the morning was over. Ethan knew that much about Lockwood, Wyoming.

He just hoped Skye and Bear Killer would stay out of sight. The woman wasn't much for taking orders, but they had talked it out this morning, and he thought there was a mutual agreement she should stay in the house with the boy. In the present public climate, it was best that anyone who even remotely resembled an Indian stay clear of Lockwood. In Skye's case, the resemblance was more than remote, and Bear Killer, though not yet a man, was strong and sinewy, with his father's height, a son worthy of a chief, and an Indian certainly capable of committing the crimes he was accused of.

Bear Killer's physical appearance presented another problem: there wasn't much chance that a Lockwood jury would see him as a helpless innocent. No, he could write off any emotional appeal from the start. The emotions were all stacked in favor of the other side. He was going to have to ferret out un-contradicted facts if Lockwood was not going to be embroiled in the middle of a Sioux Indian war.

The fools, why couldn't they see it? Why did people have to be so hellbent on self-destruction?

12

THE OAK DOOR to the sheriff's office creaked on rusty hinges as Ethan opened it and stepped in. Sheriff Will Bridges was leaning back in his chair, his booted feet propped on the desk. The sheriff, a bearish, white-haired man with pale blue eyes looked up and tipped back his battered Stetson. "Morning, Ethan," he said amiably. "Wondered when you'd be around."

"Your hinges need oil," Ethan said.

"That's my warning system," the sheriff replied. "Nobody sneaks up on me that way. Hell, if it wasn't for the squeaking hinges, you'd have caught me napping. This way I had a chance to get my eyes open before you got in."

Will Bridges played the lazy county sheriff role. Ethan knew better. The law was his life, and behind the hick facade lay a shrewd, deductive mind and an iron will. Nobody owned Will Bridges. If there was a man who didn't have a price, Sheriff Bridges would be the one. But Will Bridges was only one man, and that one man's gun was slower now. He could not rule by fear like he no doubt had in countless small Kansas and Nebraska towns in the years before he took the job in Lockwood and vowed he was there to stay.

Ethan sat down in front of the sheriff's desk and sighed. "How much do you know?"

The sheriff locked his fingers behind his neck, and his eyes met Ethan's. "That some of the good citizens of Lockwood had a lynching party while I was gone. That my so-called ex-deputy looked on while a mob murdered two Indian kids. That you took it upon yourself to haul the bodies out of Lockwood and that nobody's seen hide nor hair of you since. Enos Fletcher said he had a hunch you were headed to Lame Buffalo's camp. If you did, it's some kind of miracle you're here to tell about it."

"Not bad, so far," Ethan said. "Is that all?"

"No. I also know that we got some grave robbers hereabouts. Somebody dug up the Harpers. Their bodies are gone. That makes for interesting speculation, doesn't it?

"Well, I have a confession to make, Will. Before I left, I sent Ben Dobbs down to the Harper place to see what he could find out. He was going to dig up the bodies—"

"You mean Ben took them?"

"No. I don't think so anyway. Ben's dead."

The Sheriff swung his feet off the desk and sat upright in his chair. "The hell you say. How'd it happen?"

Ethan related the story of his homecoming and told Bridges about the attack he and Skye dePaul had aborted in the mountains.

"Son of a bitch," the sheriff exclaimed after Ethan had finished his story. "I don't believe it. It doesn't make sense. Not a damn bit. And you say Gideon Webb's name was mentioned by the gunslingers?"

"Not specifically. The only name Skye heard was 'Webb'."

"There are two Webbs, you know," the sheriff said. "Don't rule out that no account son of Gid's, Clete. He's a bad apple. Something like this is more his style."

"I hadn't forgotten about Clete, but he doesn't control the pocket book, does he?" Ethan asked. "And gunslingers don't come cheap."

"You're right there," Bridges agreed. "Gid learned the hard way a long time ago not to let loose of the money where that kid was concerned. But murder. I'd never buy that notion about Gid. He's a good man. . . . A damn fine citizen of our county. I've got to admit though, a couple of things add up."

"Like what?"

"For one, Gid's got some gunslingers hanging around the Circle W. I wouldn't rule out one of them types killed the Harpers over something—wouldn't take much to rile somebody like that, I suppose."

"What's Webb doing with gunhands?"

"You've heard about his rustling problems?"

"Yeah, I've picked up some talk. Seems like nobody else has had any trouble."

"Well, Gid's been fightin' this for better than a year, and he hadn't been none too pleased with the progress I'd made, so he went out and hired his own help. We quarreled some about it, but it's his right. Anyhow, there's hired guns available on the Circle W right now, that's for damn sure."

"You said there were a *couple* of things that added up."

"Well, you wondered how anybody could have found out what you and this gal had in mind, going up to Lame Buffalo's camp. Hell, you know how cozy Gid Webb is with Kate Wyeth."

"Miss Wyeth?" Ethan replied with genuine surprise. "Tell me

about it."

"Can't understand how you never knew. Gid and your Miss Wyeth have been keeping company for more than a year now. Gid doesn't put up at the hotel anymore when he stays in Lockwood. He drops his bedroll at Kate's house. From all indications, I'd say there's still a pretty hot fire burning in that sixty-five-year-old oven. He wouldn't be staying the night if he was just stopping by for a cup of tea."

"But Miss Wyeth? She seems so unlikely. I always thought of her being a confirmed old maid. Certainly not the shacking-up kind. I have to confess, though, she and I have never been very close."

"Hell, Ethan, she's only human. Abstinence just ain't the natural way of things. J can't believe anybody wants to go through life alone. Hell, look at me. I'm about as much of a loner as anybody you'll find, but I've got my Sarah at home and I'd damn near die without her." He paused. "You've been alone long enough, too, Ethan. It's not good for a man to be alone. It's time you were finding the right woman, somebody to settle down with."

Ethan ignored the sheriff's remarks. Will and Sarah had been matchmaking with a vengeance ever since he had come to Lockwood. A partnership like Will's and Sarah's was mighty enticing, but he would rather take on the whole Sioux nation than get caught up in a marriage war like some he'd seen.

Katherine Wyeth and Gideon Webb. He found it hard to believe. On the other hand, he supposed Gideon Webb was still a handsome, virile-looking man by most standards, and he wore that aura of strength and power that money seemed to give a man. And if you could overlook her occasional bitchiness, Miss

Wyeth was not all that unattractive, either. He suddenly saw his secretary in another light. She was a human being, a woman, apparently with a woman's needs.

"I'll talk to Miss Wyeth, Will, when I get over to the office. If I find out anything, I'll stop back here before I leave town. Now, what shall I do about Bear Killer? Can he stay out at the ranch with me until this blows over or until we need his testimony?"

"I don't think so, Ethan. I think he ought to be brought into custody."

"But, Will," Ethan protested, "those Indian boys didn't kill anybody. I know it. . . . You do, too."

"Maybe," the sheriff said, "but the folks around here are hot as hell. This town's sitting on a load of dynamite just waiting for somebody to light the fuse. If it doesn't look like something's being done, pretty soon we'll have a bunch of cowboys getting tanked up and heading for the hills for some good old Sioux hunting. They'll either get themselves killed or slaughter some squaws and Indian kids. Either way, everybody loses. If we have the boy in jail here, it shows we're doing something. It will keep folks home. We can hold off filing charges for a few days. I just have me a hunch that whatever's going to happen is going to happen fast. . . . Damn fast, maybe."

"But I vouched for the boy's safety," Ethan said. "If anything happens to Bear Killer, Lockwood's going to be a pile of ashes."

"I know that, Ethan. Look, I'll put the kid in the cell back there, feed him good. And I'll move in here myself till this is over. I'll see if I can hire some special deputies. We still got a few good men around that won't go for lynching. . . . More than you might think. The big mouths have had their day so far. I've been here for ten years, Ethan, and I decided to stay because of the people. Don't sell them short."

"I'm nervous as hell about this, Will, but I'm also an officer of the court and have an obligation. We brought the boy back to face up to this thing and to prevent a war. He'll come in."

"Does anybody hereabouts know the boy came with you?"

"No, I don't think so."

"Tell you what, then, let him stay at your place tonight. I'd guess you've got some palavering to do with that boy. I'll come out first thing in the morning and ride into town with you and the Indian lad. No sense in taking any chances."

"That's a good idea, Will. I'd appreciate it."

Ethan stood up to leave, and Will Bridges lifted himself out of his chair and offered his hand. The two shook hands with an iron grip. "Ethan," Will said, "you've dealt square with me. I won't forget that. Nobody's going to get that Indian boy without going over my dead body."

"That's what I'm afraid of," Ethan said as he moved to the door. "You watch out for yourself, Will. It took some damn tough hombres to nail Ben Dobbs."

The sheriff's face was grim. "I know, and I will watch out. We'd all better. I'll walk down the street a ways with you, Ethan. I'd better go down and break up the Enos Fletcher Show. I'll see what I can find out about the dead man. Maybe I'll have something for you if you stop back." He shook his head in disbelief as he followed Ethan out the door. "You say that woman shot this buzzard? God damn, what next? She must be one hell of a woman."

"She's one hell of a something, all right," Ethan agreed.

He had glossed over Skye dePaul's role in the mountain

massacre; he wondered what Will would say if he knew how cold bloodedly Skye had cut a man's throat. That would be a tale for another day; maybe after Skye dePaul had exited from his life.

Skye dePaul leaving. Suddenly, he felt unexplainably lonely.

13

KATHERINE WYETH DID not seem surprised when Ethan walked through the door, but on the other hand, why should she? If she thought he was dead, there would be no reason to open the office; there would be no boss to pay her salary. She did not look pleased to see him, but that was nothing new—she never did. He did not think it was because she disliked him so much as she disapproved of him. She had ruled the roost in his predecessor's office. Weatherby's bouts with the bottle had required that someone else be in charge, and Miss Wyeth who had filled that void had relished the task. Ethan could not imagine the milquetoast Weatherby challenging the woman's authority once he had surrendered it.

"Good morning, Mr. Ramsey," Miss Wyeth said coldly as he closed the door behind him. "I was wondering when you would return. Several people have been asking to see you. Mrs. Thomsen is terribly anxious to go over her will with you. I think she's upset that you haven't been available."

"I'm sorry, but she may have to wait another few days. I have to give priority to another client right now."

Miss Wyeth raised her eyebrows and her lips tightened with obvious disapproval.

"Skye dePaul," he added for good measure.

"I thought as much," she said haughtily.

"Miss Wyeth," Ethan said, "I'd like you to come in my office a minute. We have something to talk about."

"Very well, Mr. Ramsey," she said, getting up from her chair and following him into his office.

She seemed not the least defensive or concerned, Ethan noted. She was miffed, probably over the neglect of his other clients and his attention to Skye dePaul's case.

When they were seated in Ethan's office, he got right to the point. "Miss Wyeth, did you tell anyone I was taking the bodies of those Indian boys to Lame Buffalo's village?"

She was silent a moment. "I'm not certain I understand."

"It's not a complicated question, but if you want me to be more specific—did you tell Gideon Webb about my trip into the mountains?"

She fidgeted in her chair and nervously twisted the amethyst ring on her finger. "I'm not sure. I may have said something."

"I've never noticed lapses in your memory before. You've always prided yourself on your good memory, so try to know for certain. It's important. Very important."

She hesitated. "Yes," she said, her voice near a whisper. "I told him."

"And did you also tell him I was planning to bring back the Indian boy?"

"Yes."

He got up and began to pace slowly back and forth, rubbing his chin thoughtfully. Then he stopped and turned back to

Katherine Wyeth. "I can't believe it. What else did you tell him?"

She stared at him, an uncomprehending expression on her face. "Only that you agreed to represent Miss dePaul and that you were going to try to prove that the Indians didn't kill the Harpers. I really didn't think—"

"Miss Wyeth, I understand that you and Gideon Webb are friends. Good friends. That's ordinarily none of my business. But it becomes my business when it almost gets me killed. And I have reason to believe that the things you told Mr Webb did just that."

The woman paled. "No," she said. "Oh, no."

"I can't say for certain, but you can help me with some honest answers. Will your loyalty to Gideon Webb interfere with that?"

She hesitated. "No. Gideon Webb, uh . . . helps erase some of my loneliness, and I do the same for him. We are not in love; there is no marriage in our future. Besides, Mr. Ramsey, I broke a client's confidence, and yours. There's no excuse for that. I'll do what I can to help make it right."

In spite of himself, Ethan found that Katherine Wyeth was earning his grudging respect. "I appreciate that. Miss Wyeth, did Gideon Webb seem more than casually interested in my whereabouts when you saw him?"

She thought about it. "Yes, there's no question about that. He came into the office just before noon after you left town with the Indian boys. He asked me to dine with him. Now that I think about it, I've never been out to lunch with him before. He . . . he always comes to my house for supper."

"I see."

"He brought up the subject of your trip," she said. "He asked where you were going with the 'dead redskins,' as he called them.

I told him. I told him everything I knew. I had looked in the file after you left the office; I know I shouldn't have said anything, but I was angry and upset. Frankly, Mr. Ramsey, I don't like Indians, and I didn't like the idea of this office representing any."

"I'm curious. A lot of people out here don't like Indians, but you seem to have a special dislike for them. There must be a reason for your feeling so strongly. Am I right?"

"Yes, Mr. Ramsey, your assumption is correct."

"Would you mind telling me why?"

Her eyes took on a distant look and she took a deep breath as if trying to summon up the right words. "I came west to marry an officer garrisoned at Fort Laramie; he was killed in the Fetterman Massacre. My dreams died with him. I had worked as a legal secretary with a firm in New York. I had planned to return East, but our stage made a stopover in Lockwood. Mr. Weatherby had a sign in his window and I inquired. He asked me to take the job, and I never left. I've come to know other men, but none ever quite measured up to my lieutenant. I finally resigned myself to being an old maid. But when Gideon Webb came along, I didn't feel like an old maid anymore. I'm sorry. I didn't mean to talk about such personal matters. My problems aren't your concern."

"Or haven't been," Ethan said gently. "But that's going to change. . . . I promise. Tell me, Miss Wyeth, did Gideon Webb seem tense or upset about anything when you talked to him?"

"I didn't think much about it at the time . . . but, yes, I'd have to say he was. Very upset. He didn't even stay to finish lunch with me. He said he'd forgotten an appointment he had. He was very apologetic about having to leave me alone in the saloon, but I understood. He's a busy man with a lot on his mind."

"Yes, it would seem so," Ethan said, with a tinge of sarcasm. "What about Cletus Webb, Gideon's boy? What do you know about him?"

"Not a great deal, except that he's Gideon's greatest heartache. Cletus is his only heir, and like too many ranchers I've seen, Gideon built everything for his son. It was like he was going to have eternal life on that ranch through Cletus. He was so concerned about the next generation, Mr. Ramsey, that Gideon forgot to live for himself. Have you ever noticed how many people we see in our business do that? Worry so much about building and saving property for children who won't appreciate it anyway, and forget how to enjoy the fruits of what they've accumulated? Some people call it generosity, unselfishness. I call it sickness."

She had said *our* business, and now that she had let down some of the barrier between them, he saw perceptiveness and sensitivity in the woman that he had never dreamed was there. But had he ever taken the time to know her or try to understand her?

"Miss Wyeth, you say Cletus was Gideon's greatest heartache. In what way?"

"Oh, nothing specific. Gideon never liked to talk about it, but sometimes when he was especially upset he'd let things slip. He worried about the young man's drinking and the tough crowd he ran with. Cletus also has a hot temper; I gather he is prone to fits of rage when he doesn't get his way. Tantrums, Gideon called them. On top of all those things, Cletus . . . how should I say it? He doesn't have much upstairs. The worst combination, Mr. Ramsey—quick temper, slow mind. Gideon would get terribly depressed when he was having problems with Cletus. It's a little ironic, I guess. I think the only problem in his whole life that Gideon hasn't been able to handle is his own son. The way Cletus has turned out is Gideon's one defeat."

"He's not the first man to have that kind of disappointment. Only a fool builds his future on someone else's life. And it's not fair to the person who has to carry that burden."

"But he's lost everything, really, because Cletus is everything to him. In spite of it all, he loves that young man and there's no room in his heart to love anyone else. He still holds out hope that somehow Cletus will turn out all right and carry on the family name, build on the empire Gideon's started. He'll die with that hope, Mr. Ramsey." She caught her breath and her eyes met Ethan's as tears streamed down her cheeks. "I'm sorry, Mr. Ramsey. Sorrier than you'll ever know. I assume you'll be wanting me to leave."

Ethan did not hesitate. "No, not necessarily. Let's give this some time and see how things work out. This is going to be Wyoming's biggest and best law firm someday, but it will take people with brains, talent and loyalty to make it that way. I need someone like you here. If it's all right with you, let's just start fresh."

She smiled nervously. She actually smiled. "I'd like to stay, Mr. Ramsey. I will, if you want me to."

"I do," he affirmed, "and as part of our fresh start, I'd like you to start calling me 'Ethan' if you don't mind."

"That's fine Mr. . . ." she smiled, "Ethan. And I'd be pleased to have you call me Kate."

14

IT WAS MID-afternoon when Ethan turned Patch up the road that led to the ranch house. He had learned a lot in the trip to town. Gideon Webb's Circle W held the key to the Harper killings; he was certain of that. Add Ben Dobbs to that list, and a couple of innocent Indian boys. How many more before it was all over?

The bushwhacker Skye had killed had been identified by the sheriff as a hired gun—Darby Slate, who had built up his reputation in Abilene and then set up business in Cheyenne. Slate's gun had been for hire to the highest bidder, but he always stayed one step ahead of the law.

Slate's partner was Ramon Sanchez—Race as he was called in Cheyenne. It was uncertain whether 'Race' was a perversion of his name or a reference to his quickness with a gun.

While Ethan was checking in at his law office, Bridges had visited with Enos Fletcher at the livery and learned that Sanchez had shown up in Lockwood with Slate a few weeks earlier. The sheriff had also talked to a drifter in the saloon who had heard of both men. According to the man, Race was fast as a rattlesnake to strike, but unlike the reptile, hit without warning. He never gave a man an edge, and rarely an even break, according to Will's informant, but it had not hurt his reputation.

Darby Slate had killed for money. Race, evidently, killed for the love of killing and the notoriety that came with it. That helped explain why their partnership, in contrast to most gunfighting tandems, had been successful for several years.

Yes, some of the pieces were starting to fit together, but there were still a lot of unanswered questions. What did happen the night of the Harper massacre and how did the Circle W fit in? What had become of the Harper bodies? Where was Red Horse, Skye's Pawnee friend, who presumably had been with Ben Dobbs when the Harper bodies were exhumed—again assuming that Ben and Red Horse had gotten that far? Of course, it was possible that Red Horse was dead, too, his body rotting somewhere in the foothills. On a scorching day like this one, the buzzards would be picking his bones clean, and by the time the Pawnee's remains were found, there would be nothing left to prove the cause of his death.

How would Skye and Bear Killer react to his message that the Indian youth would have to be surrendered into the hands of the sheriff? He would have to remind Skye that it had been her idea, the initial reason for their trek to Lame Buffalo's village.

Damn, she could be fierce when she wanted to be. But gentle and womanly, too. He had seen that side of her. He wondered what surprises she had in store for him next. He would find out soon enough.

Patch whinnied as they neared the corrals, and he was answered by the shrill call of another horse and then another and another. "What in the hell?" Ethan murmured, as he dismounted and led his Appaloosa up to the corral. There were a dozen horses there, including several wild ones Ben had caught and the three Appaloosa mares he had purchased from Nez Perce Indians in the Palouse River country and brought all the way from central Idaho. He smiled broadly. He had almost forgotten about his prized Appaloosas. If he could locate the big stud horse, he would still have the seed stock for his herd.

He led Patch to the north corral where they had left the other horses. Razorback was gone, and so was the paint that Bear Killer had ridden down from the mountains. He unsaddled Patch and turned him loose in the corral and hurried to the house where he found the answer he had anticipated. Skye and Bear Killer were gone. Damn, what was she up to now?

His question was answered by the thunder of hooves outside, and he wheeled and went back out onto the porch. Skye and Bear Killer galloped into the ranch yard in a cloud of dust. Skye waved. "Open the corral gate, Ethan! Hurry, we are having trouble with this stallion."

Ethan dashed across the yard for the gate and swung it open. Skye and the Indian boy, weaving and cutting their horses expertly, drove in two gray mares and the Appaloosa stallion. Momentarily, they dismounted, and Bear Killer led the horses to the corral.

Ethan, hands jammed in his hip pockets, walked up to Skye who smiled brightly as she brushed wisps of damp, black hair away from her forehead. Gray dust caked her face and her clothes were sweat-soaked, but somehow she still looked very alluring. He shrugged as he came up to her. "I don't know whether to thank you or cuss," he said.

"There is no thank you owed," she said, "but why would you

be angry with us? Did you not want your horses back?"

"Damn right I wanted the horses back. I've got to have them if I'm going to make it here. You even picked up a few I didn't have before. I hope they're not a neighbor's."

"There are no brands on them. They are wild ones. . . . Probably from the same herd where you got the other wild horses. They are good ones, though; we let a few of the others go. If you are going to build a herd, you want the best. You require more than the few Appaloosas right now to build this ranch. These are strong and have tremendous stamina. You'll eventually want more Appaloosas, though. My uncle has stolen many of them from the Nez Perce and the Blackfoot. Very few white men are raising them, but in a short time, when people learn more about these horses, you will have a ready market."

"I'm glad I have your approval," he said sardonically. "Skye, I truly am grateful for what you did, but it wasn't a wise thing to do with circumstances the way they are. . . . The hostility against the Sioux is too great right now. What if someone had seen you? Taken a shot at you or Bear Killer? Or worse yet, killed you? You could run into trouble with people who would normally be friendly, let alone whoever's been trying to do us in."

"There was nothing to worry about," she said nonchalantly. "We did not let anyone see us. We stayed in our cage most of the morning, but it was too much for us to endure. We had to do something, and I knew you had lost your horses. You would not have lost them if you had not agreed to help us, and I was afraid you would increase your fees to purchase new ones." A smile crossed her lips, and he found it hard to remain cool to the warm sparkle of her eyes.

"All right," he said, "you win. Why don't you and Bear Killer go on up to the house? I'll get some fresh water from the well. You can have a cool drink and wash up if you want."

"Thank you, Ethan, I would like that. But first, there is something else I thought I might mention."

"What's that?"

"I saw cattle with the Lazy R brand in the valley. I assume they are yours."

"They were Ben's Longhorns; I guess they're mine now."

"Those cattle will not thrive in this country; they are more suited for the plains of Texas and Oklahoma."

"I know that," he said, irritation in his voice, "but there aren't many other cattle in this part of the country. You take what you can buy. I've studied cattle a lot. There's an English breed—Herefords, they call them—which I think would do well in Wyoming. They're very hardy and fast-growing. Meatier than a Longhorn. One of my dreams is to import some of those cattle, but that's a long way off."

"Have you thought of Durhams?" she asked. "They have many of the qualities of the Hereford cattle."

"I know a little about them. The ranchers I know call them shorthorns, but I don't know of any in this part of the country."

"I know where there are some in Kansas," she said. "Before I came here, I taught at a Quaker school about fifty miles north of Dodge City. A rancher there was establishing a Durham herd. Three or four years ago, he already had a small purebred herd, and if things went well, he should be selling breeding stock by now. I could provide you with his name and address if you like. A Durham bull with your Longhorn cows would do a great deal to upgrade your herd. If you could get some purebred cows, you might even get a head start on the Durham market in

Wyoming."

If he gave her another week, she would take over the whole damn ranch. But she was right, he admitted to himself. Ethan set aside his pride. "I'd like his name and address. Sounds like a good idea. Where did you learn so much about ranching?"

"My father had a small ranch near Cheyenne. Although we did not live on it, we spent much time there. I love horses and cattle and have read a lot about ranching. Wherever I taught, I always visited the ranches to find out what they were doing. I went to schools in Indiana and Kansas before returning here, so I worked my way back west, so to speak, and had an opportunity to see some of the cattle developments that are taking place in the east. This is truly cattle country, but our ranchers here could learn a great deal from the cattlemen further east if they were predisposed to do so."

"Well, you're the last person I expected to be a teacher of agricultural science, but I'm willing to learn about anything you've picked up along the way."

"You are a different man, Ethan."

"What do you mean?"

"Most men I have met would resent a woman offering the suggestions I have made."

"Why did you offer them if you thought I might resent it?"

"I do not know. Perhaps, I was testing you."

"Why?"

"I do not know. . . . I will have to think about that."

15

BEAR KILLER HAD been like a shadow since their first meeting, silent and in the background, yet ever present. It was hard to tell what the boy was thinking. From the time Lame Buffalo had abruptly and unceremoniously surrendered the boy just before their departure from the village, Bear Killer's solemn face had been set in stone. His black eyes were alert and intelligent, but they revealed nothing of the uncertainty and turmoil that had to be eating away at the boy's guts. He understood English, for Skye spoke to him constantly in the language, but he always responded with a nod or some other silent gesture . . . at least in Ethan's presence. Alone with Skye, the boy, no doubt, spoke. He was surprisingly at home in the ranch house, and now they sat at the supper table, quietly eating the beef stew and biscuits Ethan and Skye had prepared together. It occurred to Ethan that Bear Killer must have had some experience in the white man's world. Although he held his spoon awkwardly, he held it properly, and his table manners were more socially acceptable than those of many white boys Ethan had encountered on the frontier.

Ethan suspected that in spite of his protests, Lame Buffalo

foresaw that a new way of life was inevitable for the Sioux, and that the father was preparing his son to make a place in the new order of things. Ethan had not noticed it before, but the wily Sioux Chief had even employed a lawyer's trick: he had dressed the client for his performance. Bear Killer, in his pilgrimage from the mountains, had not worn the scanty breech cloth of a savage Indian boy. He had been attired in a buckskin shirt and denim trousers, and, shorn of his shoulder-length hair, he would have looked very civilized indeed.

Sheriff Bridges would be out in the morning to escort Bear Killer back to Lockwood. Before he did, Ethan needed to ask the Indian boy some questions. He was curious about this young man, and perhaps Bear Killer could shed further light on the events that had taken place on the night of the Harper killings.

The sun slipped behind the mountains, and the room darkened as they finished eating. Ethan lit the kerosene lamp and placed it in the center of the table, but set it dim so they would not be easy targets for some bushwhacker outside.

Skye got up and retrieved the huge, black coffee pot from its perch above the fireplace. "More coffee, Ethan?" she asked, and without waiting for a reply, she filled his tin cup before she filled her own. Then she sat down and touched her lips gingerly to the steaming cup. "Hot," she remarked, after taking a sip.

"Yes, it is," he replied, stroking his own cup absent-mindedly.

"Ethan?"

"Yes."

"Are you going to tell us what happened in town today? I thought I might have received a report from my lawyer by now. If you had good news, I think you would have said something."

"We've been too busy to talk ever since I got back. Somebody rounded up my horses and got this ranch back in business, remember?" He hesitated. "But you're correct; I have been putting it off. I'll give you the important news first."

"What is that?"

Ethan turned to Bear Killer. "Sheriff Bridges wants to take Bear Killer into custody. He's coming out in the morning to ride into town with us."

The boy's face was expressionless. "Did you expect otherwise?" Skye asked.

"No, but I hoped otherwise. Bear Killer," Ethan said, turning to the boy, "we haven't had a chance to talk. If I'm going to help you, I need to know more about you, and I need to ask some questions."

The boy looked at Skye who smiled faintly and nodded reassuringly. His eyes met Ethan's unflinchingly. "I will speak with you," he said softly in clear, precise English.

"You have spent time among the white man. . . . Tell me about it."

"There is little to tell. As a small child, I made many visits to Cheyenne to stay in the lodge of my aunt, Singing Lark. Although I did not want to, my cousin, Sky-in-the-Morning, made me learn the white man's tongue."

"He can read English, too," Skye interjected with obvious pride. "Very well. He is probably the only boy in the whole Sioux nation who keeps books wrapped in his buffalo robe."

"Does your father approve?" Ethan asked.

"No, I think not," the boy said. "He wishes me to be a great warrior."

"I think you are wrong," Skye said, "He has encouraged your education. It was he who asked if you might spend the winter at the Quaker school last year. He wishes for his son not only to be a great warrior, but for his son to be a great chief, one who can lead his people in the world that is coming. That will require knowledge beyond what you can acquire living in your father's village. He knows this, believe me, but he cannot openly admit it, for his people are not ready to accept it. He is preparing you to lead. Remember, that is what leaders do—they lead. They must go first and break the trail."

Bear Killer seemed not to hear Skye's words. "Do not judge all Sioux women by my cousin, Mr. Ramsey. My father says she does not know her place. But he says when she succeeds in capturing the Puma, he will quickly plant his seed and put her to the woman's work of raising cubs."

Taken aback and suddenly ill at ease, Ethan cast a glance at Skye whose dark eyes flashed with anger.

"That . . . that is a stupid thing to say," Skye snapped, obviously embarrassed and flustered. "What would Lame Buffalo say if he knew that his son spoke with a forked tongue?"

The boy grinned broadly, evidently pleased that he had riled Skye. Ethan did not know what to say and decided it was best to say nothing and let the two antagonists settle their dispute in their own way.

"My father would say I speak the truth, my cousin. You do not know why I am here? It is because my father went to the place of dreams the night you entered our village. He did not want me to go with you, but he had a vision—"

"Vision," Skye scoffed, "Everybody has visions. We call them dreams. White men call bad ones nightmares; they have nothing to do with real life."

Ethan thought that Skye's disavowal lacked conviction.

"That is not true," Bear Killer insisted, "and you know it is not. The part of you that is Sioux believes in dreams and cannot deny them. You are afraid to hear of my father's vision," he taunted.

"Tell me your vision, papoose."

Bear Killer looked smug. "My father waited in the place of dreams, but nothing came but the sounds of the night and the wind from the mountains. The stars began to fade from the skies and my father feared the Great Spirit had been called to other work and would not help him in his time of trial. Then a coyote he-dog called to his mate from the far end of the valley, and the she-dog answered from somewhere above the cave where my father sat. My father's eyes closed and the vision came."

"You speak much and say little," Skye chided.

Bear Killer ignored her and continued. "In his dream, my father saw a river, the flat water—the Platte, the white man calls it. On one side stood warriors of our village painted for war and armed for battle. On the other, were the blue-coated yellow-legs. They, too, were prepared for war. My father raised his arm to signal his warriors to attack, when from among the yellow-legs appeared the Puma. He waded into the shallow flat water and crossed it to where our people stood. Standing before my father, he held out his arm and cut his own wrist with his knife. The blood flowed like milk from the tits of a nursing mare, so my father said. And then, as if from nowhere, you, my cousin, Sky-in-the-Morning, appeared beside the Puma. You took his knife, cut your arm and pressed your bleeding flesh against his, and your blood mixed. And when my father looked again across the river, the yellow-legs were turning their horses away from this place that had been chosen for battle. Then the Puma took my cousin's hand and led her to the water, and they walked away to follow his people. My father turned to the Brule, and said, 'Return to your lodges; we shall fight the white man no more.'"

Ethan could see at the conclusion of his story that the boy was tense, wet with cold sweat, in as emotional a state as he had ever seen a Sioux male. The boy had not invented the story for the purpose of annoying Skye. Bear Killer believed in this dream, and he believed in the message it carried. Ethan shivered involuntarily; he did not know what to believe, but the boy's story was unsettling as hell.

Skye, too, was visibly shaken by what the boy had related. She got up from her chair and with trembling hands began to remove the plates and utensils from the table. An awkward silence consumed the room. It was as though a spell had been cast upon them, and no one dared break it.

This was not a tongue-tied boy as he had originally suspected. This was an eloquent young man, as intelligent as any he had seen among any people. Among the whites, he would have been tagged as a future politician. There was no doubt in Ethan's mind that Bear Killer had the soul of a great statesman. And this was a boy whom he was to deliver into the hands of a sheriff who, try as he may, might not be able to ward off fanatical, irrational whites who had a taste for Sioux blood. Any Sioux blood.

Was he surrendering a young Lincoln or budding Jefferson for slaughter? His task had been much easier, less conscience-rending, before he had so abruptly come to know and sense the spirit of the boy.

Ethan tensed as he heard the door squeak behind him. Reflexively, his hand darted for his pistol, and he wheeled. Then he saw Skye was leaving the house, and he relaxed.

The spell broken, Ethan spoke. "Bear Killer, if you wish, I will return you to the village of your father. You don't have to go with Sheriff Bridges tomorrow. We can leave for your village tonight."

"No," the boy said. "My father says we must settle this in the white man's way. It was you who told him this. Have you acquired some new wisdom that would change your mind? No, my head tells me this is what we must do." He clenched his fist to his chest, "But my heart does not want to."

"I can't guarantee your safety, Bear Killer. I may have promised too much to your father."

"I will go. My father says that the Puma, the lawyer, is sent by the Great Spirit to speak for our people in the councils of the white eyes, and that I am to be a symbol of our trust in your wisdom. He came to know this on the night of the coyote."

Ethan shook his head in disbelief. "That's a mighty big load you just put on my shoulders, Bear Killer. But yes, I think we'd better ride in with Sheriff Bridges tomorrow. Now, before we call it a day, I have some questions about the night Jake Harper and his daughter were killed."

"If I can answer, my cousin, I shall."

Crazy damn kid. This was all moving too fast. He already had him in the family. He hated like hell to disillusion the boy right now with all he had to face these next few days, but marriage to Skye dePaul would be like being married to two women—she'd put you to bed with a prayer, and wake you up with a scalping knife. Besides, beautiful as she was, he could not see Skye dePaul as the marrying kind. On the other hand, before tonight, he had never thought of himself as the marrying kind. He didn't want to think about Skye dePaul at all right now.

"Bear Killer, the night your friends were lynched and you escaped, were you anywhere near the Harper place?"

"I don't know."

"What do you mean, you don't know?"

"I do not know where the Harper place is, so I cannot know if I was near the place. If you mean, did we attack a white family and kill them—no. We did not see anything, and we did not hear anything until the white men came to our camp and took us away."

"What were you doing this near Lockwood?"

"In the winter, I lived at the Quaker school. I helped with milking of the cows and cared for the livestock owned by the Quakers. I went to class with the white students. Some of them were not pleased that an Indian came to their school, but others became friends. Screeching Hawk and Raven Eyes came with me to visit one of my white friends, Jamie Carlson. We stayed at his father's ranch for a day."

"Charlie Carlson?"

"Yes, that is his name."

Ethan knew Charlie Carlson. He was a small rancher who had the C Bar C spread a few miles west of the Webb place. Charlie was a good man, not likely to be intimidated by his neighbor. If he could vouch for the Indian boys' presence at his ranch, it would show they had good cause for being in the vicinity. He made a mental note to ride out to Charlie's place and verify the story.

"Did you carry any weapons?"

"Our knives and bows. We hoped to return to the village with meat. Some in our village did not think my father should permit us to make the journey. We thought it might stop their grumbling if we returned with meat . . . but instead, we brought only death, and some of the people are doubting my father's wisdom as chief."

"Like Badger Claw, for instance?"

"Yes. How did you know?"

"A lucky guess." So the Indians had their political power struggles, too.

"Some think I was a coward for not staying with my friends, but we all tried to break free. The others were caught. My pony was faster."

And you were smarter, Ethan thought.

"There was nothing I could do. At the time I did not know they planned to kill my friends. I thought they would be put in the white man's jail, and I did not know what we were accused of."

"You did the right thing, Bear Killer. There's a big difference between being foolish and being brave. Would you recognize any of the men who captured you?"

"It was dark. But two, I will never forget. One, they called the deputy, told the others he was in charge, but they treated him as buffalo dung. He was a weak man and a coward. The true leader was a huge man, broad and tall as the grizzly, fierce and angry. The others feared him but did not respect him. It was he who demanded our death. It was he who first called us murderers, savages."

"But did you not hear his name?"

"No, but I would know him."

The description could fit a lot of people—including Clete Webb. All roads led to the Circle W; that would be where the answers would be found. . . . If at all.

The door to the ranch house opened and Skye stepped in, followed by a stocky, gray-haired Indian dressed in white man's attire from the black Plainsman hat on his head to the scuffed leather boots on his feet.

Ethan got up and extended his hand. The Indian nodded solemnly and accepted it. "Red Horse, you are one man we're mighty glad to see," Ethan said. "Sit down, please."

"Pour Red Horse some coffee, Ethan," Skye said. "I will heat up the leftover stew and biscuits. This poor man has not eaten anything but berries and roots for three days."

The Pawnee took a chair. In the soft lamplight, Ethan could see that the Indian was very old, for his face was crisscrossed with a web of creases that looked like they had been carved there. But he was a barrel-chested man and his muscular arms and shoulders were evidence he was far from feeble.

Skye talked as she knelt at the fireplace and stirred the stew in the Dutch oven. "Red Horse was with Ben Dobbs at the Harper place the night after we left Lockwood. He knows who killed Ben; they tried to kill him, too. Apparently, someone was afraid they were going to find something there. Red Horse has been hiding in the hills between here and the Pennock School waiting for one of us to show up. He is one Pawnee who can count coup on a Sioux, believe me. I was walking along the edge of the trees when he came up from behind me out of nowhere."

"You're lucky it was Red Horse," Ethan scolded. "That's why you should keep your damn fool head in the house. You're not invincible; none of us are."

"You always know what's best, don't you?"

"I've never suggested such a thing. I learned better a long time ago. I consider myself lucky if I'm right half the time."

"If you are no better than that, perhaps I should get another lawyer."

"The way this has turned out, I wish you had. Ben Dobbs would be alive today."

She stared up at him, a hurt look on her face, eyes like those of a puppy that had just been swatted. Damn, he hadn't meant to say that. He wasn't blaming her; he was just so damn frustrated with all that had happened, and the loss of Ben was only now beginning to sink in. He hurt, too. He hurt like hell, and working the Lazy R was going to be lonely as the devil without Ben around.

Ethan swallowed hard. "I didn't mean that, Skye. I'm upset about things. I'm sorry."

"It is all right," she said softly and then turned back to the stew. "But it is true, I guess."

Ethan prided himself on his even, cautious temperament. He was not given to shooting from the hip and had not had to take back many words in his life. He wished he could take back the last ones. For some reason, it was important to him that he not hurt Skye dePaul.

He turned to Red Horse who had been watching Skye and Ethan with interest throughout their exchange. "Well, Red Horse, my first question is who killed Ben Dobbs?"

The Pawnee held up two fingers. "Two men. Strangers who wear guns low. One taller, skinny fellow . . . older than you, maybe. Never seen before."

"Probably the same hombres who were waiting to ambush us," Ethan said, as Skye placed a plate of stew and biscuits in front of the Pawnee. "One's dead; the other will be soon."

The Indian swiped a biscuit through the beef broth, and

stuffed it in his mouth and chomped and sucked noisily before he swallowed and then spoke. "Ben Dobbs and me, we went to the Harper farm before sundown. Damn stupid. Ben wanted to read sign. We went everyplace around the yard. . . . No injun sign. Ben Dobbs knew injun sign. I know Sioux sign. No injun sign. We got plenty of white sign. Shod horses all over hell. Boots; everybody wears boots. No moccasin prints. If Sioux been there more than three nights past, I smell them." He looked at Skye and Bear Killer and shrugged. "Damn sorry, but true. Not bad smell, but I know Sioux."

"Okay, so you didn't find anything," Ethan said. "Then what happened?"

"Started to leave. Ben wanted to come back after dark to dig up bodies. But Circle W riders rode in. Should run like hell, but too damn stupid. Ben Dobbs said wait. So we wait. Four riders come up. Madder than damn hell. Clete Webb with them; told us to get the hell out. Ben Dobbs said 'you get the hell out'. Clete was ready to draw, then seen my scatter gun pointed at his belly. They rode away first. We went into the hills to wait for sundown." The Pawnee stopped and returned to his eating. He devoured the rest of his food and downed a cup of coffee while Ethan waited impatiently.

Then Red Horse continued. "After dark comes, we ride back in. Damn stupid. White spirits; Indians spirits—no difference. Don't like it. I told Ben Dobbs, damn stupid. Ben said 'go back to goddamn school, then'. I stayed. Damn sorry, too. Not hard to dig up, just covered with little dirt and rocks. Both of them—father and daughter. Damn bad deal . . . damn bad."

"Could you tell anything?"

"Not much. . . . Enough."

"Well, what?"

"It was dark, moonlight bright, but still damn dark."

"Well, what did you find out, Red Horse?"

"Jake shot. Shot through his damn chest."

"Scalped?"

"Nope."

"Mutilated?"

"Mu—"

"Mutilated. Cut up. . . . Chopped up. . . . With a knife or axe."

"No, not that. Shot in chest. Pistol, Ben said. Shot up close. I don't know. Don't read guns good."

Ethan looked at Bear Killer. "You said you didn't have any guns that night, right?"

"No. Boys our age? There are not many rifles in our village. No pistols. Do you think my father would let boys take our few guns?"

"No, of course not. It's just the lawyer in me. . . . I wanted to confirm it. To hear what you would say. It's a good answer. One that makes sense. The kind I like to hear on the witness stand."

Ethan turned back to Red Horse. "What about the girl?"

"Too dark, couldn't tell. Not shot. Not stabbed. No time to find out."

"What do you mean?"

"Ben and me took Jake and the girl into hills, then go back and cover empty graves. Damn crazy. Riders come again. More riders . . . six, seven maybe. We didn't wait to see. Plenty damn scared. Ben and me buried bodies in gully. Covered with rocks. Bad not to bury dead. Spirits all over hell. Ben said he didn't want nobody digging them up. Who want to?"

"There might be somebody," Ethan said. "Ben knew what he was doing. Can you find the place again?"

The Indian cocked his head and stared at Ethan. "Damn stupid question."

"Red Horse, you've given me a lot of good information. Your testimony might not prove who's guilty, but it will go a hell of a long way toward proving the Indian boys were innocent . . . if the jury will listen."

Skye warmed Red Horse's coffee, and he grunted something akin to thank you. "Cynthia Harper," Skye asked, "what was she wearing?"

"Not damn much."

"A dress? A gown? What?"

Red Horse gulped down the cup of coffee and held out the cup for a refill. The Pawnee stared at his coffee cup, seemingly embarrassed by the questions. "Underthings. Damn little of them."

"Were they torn or anything like that?" Ethan asked.

Red Horse shook his head negatively.

Ethan's immediate thought was that Cynthia Harper might have been attacked and raped. Her father could have been killed trying to stop the assault. Murder was never logical, but the theory, or some variation of it, was plausible. It was something to think on.

"Red Horse," Ethan said, "I'm still not sure when Ben got killed. Near as I can tell, he must have been killed the day after Skye and I left for Lame Buffalo's village."

"Night, I think. The two rattlesnakes come to the Quaker School next morning. Miss McBride call me up to school building, said somebody wants talk to me. I went; seen damn rattlesnakes waiting there. Older fellar said Ben Dobbs wanted to see me, hurt bad. Said they was friends of his and would ride to his place with me. Thought I was damn dumb injun, that's what they thought. . . . Damn dumb injun. Said I get my horse. Went back to barn and got my horse, all right. Then beat the hell out back door. Damn gunslingers, that's what they was. Rattlesnakes. Killed me deader than hell, if I let them. Not such a damn dumb injun. Seventy-five winters I've lived. Damn dumb injuns don't live that long, not in these mountains."

"Did they follow you?"

"Oh, you betcha. I circle round Lockwood, came out on top of Lazy R and seen damn buzzards in sky. Go down closer and seen Ben Dobbs in the yard . . . dead, damn dead. Seen that. Then heard rattlesnakes coming from down trail and got hell out. Had to leave Ben Dobbs for worms. Felt damn bad, and now Ben Dobbs' spirit madder than hell, too." The Pawnee, his face stoic, shrugged. "Nothing else to say. Been keeping red ass in trees ever since. Figured if you wasn't scalped, you or Miss Skye show up sooner or later."

"These gunslingers," Ethan said, "the rattlesnakes, you ever see them before?"

"Hell, no. Don't forget them kind. Damn hired guns."

Ethan sat quietly, gazing pensively at the flickering lamp. Then he looked at the Pawnee. "Red Horse, how are you with a gun?"

"Pistol, no damn good. Rifle okay. Scatter-gun, damn good."

"I think Will Bridges could use a man who can handle a shotgun," Ethan said. "The sheriff's coming out in the morning to take Bear Killer into protective custody. I'd like you to go along for two reasons. First, you're a key witness, probably the most important one we've got. You'll be safer in town with the sheriff. Secondly, I have a hunch the sheriff is going to come up short-handed on getting help to guard the jail. If you can handle a shotgun, you could make a difference if there's trouble at the jail. But I have to warn you, it could be a very dangerous place to be."

"If there's place to sleep and food to eat, I'll go," the Pawnee said. "Tired of eating like a damn buffalo."

16

ETHAN TWISTED HIS neck and tugged at the stiff shirt collar that chafed uncomfortably at his skin. He felt like some eastern city dude in his gray suit and black string tie. The days out of the office, dressed in simple, open-necked garments had spoiled him, and as he thumbed through the neatly-written memoranda Katherine Wyeth had left on his desk, he wondered, not for the first time, if he was truly suited for the legal profession. Somehow, it was difficult to see his destiny in the drab prison of these four walls.

It was Wednesday. He had assured Katherine she could start making appointments for his clients—if he still had any—next week. He was certain that no matter what happened, his role in the Harper murders would bring him back to the town's stream of life by then.

Already he was laying the groundwork for whatever legal battle lie ahead. This morning, they had gotten Bear Killer settled in a cell. Red Horse had moved into the jail's only other cell next to the Sioux boy. Ethan found the presence of the old Pawnee and the big double-barreled shotgun he cradled so menacingly in his arms reassuring. Will Bridges seemed glad enough to accept the Pawnee's help and had told Ethan it was his plan to move his own personal things into the front office and plant himself on the old cot there until the Harper business was resolved.

Red Horse, of course, was not a prisoner. The boy's cell would be left unlocked, too, Will had said. Just in case somebody did get through over his dead body, he was not going to have the Indian boy cornered like a rat in a trap. Will knew that Bear Killer was innocent and that there was no way a white man would have been held on the flimsy evidence, but like Ethan, the wily old sheriff knew they were playing for the bigger stakes of averting a bloody Indian war.

Ethan was to meet with Bridges and the town council at the sheriff's office later this morning. "I need some help," Will had said. "I kicked Rube Tatnall out on his ass. I'm not sure he shouldn't be in the hoosegow for malfeasance in office, or something. But now, I don't have a deputy. I'd like to get Red Horse deputized, give him a little more weight. But did you ever hear of an Indian deputy in Wyoming?" Without waiting for an answer, Bridges continued, "They're all well-meaning old farts, but they're scared shitless right now. They're afraid the town's going to go up in smoke. But we still need the council's backing to get the decent people behind us. You have a way with folks, Ethan. Somehow, what you say always sounds reasonable. A good law wrangler might help me out with those gents. You can't do any harm being there, I know that."

Ethan had been anxious to return to the ranch, but he could see the sense in Will Bridge's pleas and agreed to be at the meeting. It was not the ranch he was worried about; it was Skye. With typical stubbornness, she had refused to join them on the trip to town. He had just assumed she would be going with them, but after breakfast, she had started to clean up the house and gave no indication she planned to go with them.

She had been strangely quiet and subdued since Bear Killer hit her with the vision story the previous night. Something sure as hell was eating at her. Maybe the Indian in her took the dream seriously; he sure as hell didn't. Not now, in the bright of day. He had heard a lot of stories about Indian visions. And a lot of Indians were dead now because they believed in the invincibility or supernatural powers bestowed upon them by their dreams.

He and the two Indians had seen to the care of the stock that morning, and as Bear Killer and Red Horse saddled up the horses in readiness for Will Bridges' arrival, Ethan returned to the house. There he found Skye serenely sweeping the floor of his combined parlor-kitchen. "Do you suppose you could get your things together?" he had asked.

She looked at him quizzically, "What for?"

"Well, Bear Killer won't be here anymore. I thought maybe you could go back to the Quaker school. You should be safe there with the other teachers. Or, if you prefer, you could put up in the hotel."

"I was planning to stay here . . . for now," she said matter-of-factly. "Unless you will not permit me."

"Don't put it that way. I thought you'd be safer someplace else. And I don't . . . well, I don't suppose it's quite proper, really . . . under the circumstances."

"What circumstances?"

"Well, a man and a woman . . . it's not like we're brother and sister. Oh, hell, do I have to spell it out?"

"You do not want me here then?"

115

"No . . . Yes . . . I want you here, but—"

"Then I shall stay. I think you will be safer if I am here."

"Good God, woman, I was Chief of Scouts at Laramie; I'm not some goddamn tenderfoot. I can take care of myself."

"I did not say you could not, but we have found on several occasions that it is safer when we are together."

"Yes," he conceded, "I can't deny that."

They had made a good team so far, he thought at the time. They seemed to have an uncanny way of anticipating what the other would think, the move the other would make. It was a little spooky.

"Well, I'd rather you didn't stay here alone," he had persisted. "Ride into town with us this morning. I have to take care of some things in the office. We can have dinner in town and come back to the ranch after that."

"There are things that need to be done here, Ethan. You do not have Ben Dobbs to check on the cattle anymore."

"I'll check them when we get back."

"Did you notice that one of the Appaloosa mares is getting ready to foal?"

"No," he admitted, "I was in a hurry this morning."

"I was out before you got up. She was showing blood already. I think she will foal later this morning. She should be moved into the barn, and someone should be here in case there is trouble. I am quite competent at such things."

"I have no doubt that you are," he had said sarcastically, "but damn it, Skye, I just don't think—"

"Go to town, Ethan," she had interrupted. "Remember, I am Sioux. I will not be surprised by any intruders."

She had turned away and gone back to work, signaling there

was nothing more to be said. He had wheeled and marched angrily out of the house, slamming the door behind him.

He sat there now, staring at the inkwell on the desk as if mesmerized by it. Skye dePaul had sure as hell got under his skin. It was getting harder and harder not to think about her, and it suddenly occurred to him that he did not want to go back to a lonely ranch, and that he was glad Skye would be there when he returned. He did not intend to eat dinner in town; he was eager to get back home.

Katherine Wyeth came into his office and brought him back from his musing. "Mr. Ramsey . . . Ethan," she said, "I saw something unusual when I glanced out of the window a little bit ago. . . . I don't know what it means."

"What's that?"

"Well, I saw Clete Webb and a couple of Gideon Webb's hands ride into town. They went into the Cottonwood Palace. I thought it strange they'd be in town in the middle of the morning this time of year, but I assumed they'd been sent in to get some supplies or something and just stopped at the saloon for a drink. Well, it's been better than half an hour now, and their horses are still tied in front of the saloon. I suppose it's nothing, but doesn't it seem a bit unusual?"

"You're thinking they could have been sent in to stir up some trouble?"

"I don't like thinking it. I feel disloyal after all Gideon and I have been to each other. But after everything you've said about the Circle W's involvement the night of the Harper killings and since, I thought I should say something. . . . I was afraid not to."

"I appreciate that, Katherine." Ethan pushed back his chair and got up. "I think I'll stop by the Palace and have a beer after I meet with the town council."

17

ETHAN SILENTLY STUDIED the men who gathered in the sheriff's office. Four of the five members of the Lockwood town council sat in the straight-backed chairs scattered about the sheriff's office. The fifth, Josh Wilson, was conspicuous by his absence. Wilson, proprietor of the town's only general store, was a long-time crony of Gideon Webb's. Besides, Ethan thought, the purchases made by Circle W would be the lifeblood of Wilson's commercial enterprises. The fact that Wilson had no competition made not a whit of difference. An outfit like the Circle W could put a competitor in business overnight.

On the other hand, the other members of the council were not that much less vulnerable to a Circle W boycott. George Caldwell, with his funeral home and furniture store and other sundry businesses, was certainly not immune to Webb pressure, and it showed. The rotund little man fidgeted in his chair and mopped the slick, shiny dome of his skull with a wrinkled handkerchief. George would much rather be fixing up a corpse for burial right now, but he was an intensely curious man. Nosey would be a better way of putting it. He had to find out what was up before he pulled his head into the shell.

The other three were more far-sighted. Dr. Henry Weintraub was a young medical doctor whose Jewishness was overlooked in the community because he was the only sawbones within fifty miles. A damned good one, too. Ethan liked to think that men like Weintraub were Lockwood's future—men of intelligence and skill, with the ambition and spirit to carve places for themselves in the heart of this wilderness. And Weintraub had a personal stake in the town—a new bride from the East was expected before summer was out, an arrangement negotiated by mail, Weintraub had confided to Ethan. An Indian war would spoil those plans, wash them away in a shower of blood. At least physicians in the West were not so expendable as merchants, not that it would make any difference to Henry. Ethan could count on the good doctor.

Cyrus Eastland would stand by young Doc Weintraub. The old gentleman with flowing white hair and a heavy mustache that glistened like the fur of a silver fox, published and edited the Lockwood Journal, the town's weekly newspaper, and did printing jobs on the side. He was writer, editor and pressman, and like most newspapermen Ethan had encountered, was fiercely independent. His common sense opinions expressed so bluntly on the Journal's editorial page had won Eastland the community's esteem. One faction or the other usually hated his guts and vilified his name the day after the Journal came out, but his viewpoint always earned grudging respect, and in person he was never the hard, uncompromising voice that spoke from the Journal. On the contrary, he was gentle and friendly, almost shy in his manner. Somehow the people of Lockwood saw Cy Eastland as two men—one, the kind, subtle-humored old gentleman who was their friend; the other, an unrelenting conscience who too often told them what they did not want to hear.

Finally, there was Herman Roebke, the massive-shouldered German blacksmith. An immigrant, blond and ruddy-complexioned, Roebke had pulled his oxen out of a wagon train heading to Oregon several years back and had driven the team and wagon into Lockwood. A few days later, he was shoeing horses on the street. In a matter of weeks, he had rented space in the back of Enos Fletcher's livery and was doing a booming business. He was now in the process of building his own shop. Roebke, in his early forties, had an equally Teutonic wife, a physically strong, buxom woman some years younger than her husband and quite attractive, seemingly unfazed by having borne six children—or was it seven by now? Roebke, too, was Lockwood's future, but where did he stand on this question? Roebke, perhaps because of his awkwardness in the language of his new country, rarely talked. He mostly smiled and nodded and spoke in a broken hybrid of English and German only when he had something important to say—which seemed to be seldom. Ethan liked the man, but who knew what the big German might be thinking? If he had things figured right, Herman Roebke's vote would be crucial.

The law required a majority of the entire five-member council to make a decision. It took three votes to commit the town to a course of action; only two could be reasonably accounted for.

Will Bridges sat behind his desk with the town council before him, but Eastland, the mayor elected by the other council members, presided. At Eastland's request, Ethan had taken a chair off to one side of the sheriff's desk, and it gave him a feeling that he and Bridges were sitting on trial before the council members.

"Will, I take it you thought it was important, or you wouldn't have asked for this special meeting. Can you tell us what you have in mind?" Eastland asked.

"Well, gentlemen," Sheriff Bridges said, "I think you have a pretty good idea what I'm up to. I know the word's out. I've got Lame Buffalo's son in jail back there. I asked Ethan to be here because he's the boy's lawyer. Now, I'll get to the point. We've got some problems. Big ones. Things have been popping faster than popcorn on a hot skillet ever since the Harpers were killed. We've already had a lynching in this town, and it makes me sick deep in my gut."

Eastland shook his head in dismay. "Barbarism. Plain, animal barbarism. That's what the editorial in tomorrow night's paper is going to say. But it won't bring those Indian boys back. Innocent or guilty, they should have had their day in court. If we can't stop that sort of thing, we'd just as well close up Lockwood, pack our bags and head back East."

"If they killed the Harpers, that's what they had coming," the undertaker interjected.

Dr. Weintraub's eyes glowered beneath dark, heavy eyebrows. "If," he said sharply, "but that's what we have courts for. To decide 'if'. In some parts of the country, they hang Jews or Negroes without taking the time to find out 'if'. I came here because I assumed that only what a man could do was important, not the color of his skin, his religion or the language he speaks."

Was Weintraub trying to make a subtle point with Roebke with his last statement?

"I think I should make it very clear, gentlemen," Bridges said, "That Indian boy is in jail for protective custody. He hasn't been charged with a damn thing yet. Frankly, I don't see how he can be. The only thing against him is that he's an Indian, and maybe we're not past the day when that's a hanging offense. The reason the boy came back was because Miss dePaul down at the Quaker school realized that if he didn't, we could be facing a new Indian war in these parts. Miss dePaul—she's Lame Buffalos' niece—and Ethan somehow managed to convince Lame Buffalo of the same thing. I don't know how the Chief can show his trust any more than by turning his own son over to the white man's law. Not sure I could do that if I was in his moccasins. Now, the way I see it, the only way we can keep the Chief's trust and stop a war is to protect his boy. If we can show we mean business, we can save a lot of lives and maybe make some new friends out in those mountains."

"So why are we here, Will?" Eastland asked.

"I want two emergency resolutions from this council. As you know, Rube Tatnall's done as my deputy, done in this town as far as I'm concerned. I've got the Pawnee from the Quaker school, Red Horse, holed up in one of the cells in back. He's an important witness in this case, but he's also agreed to help me guard . . . maybe I should say protect . . . the prisoner. I want you to pass a motion to make him deputy with all the rights and duties appertaining."

The undertaker's mouth flopped open in horror. "An Indian deputy in this town? The people won't stand for it. They'll be up in arms."

"I'm afraid some of them are going to be up in arms anyway," Bridges said. "I need a deputy. Do you want to volunteer,

George?"

"Don't be ridiculous. I'm no hand with a gun."

"Seems like the men who would handle a gun are few and far between right now," the sheriff said cynically. "But I want something else, too, gentlemen, before you act on my request. I want general authority to deputize as many citizens as necessary to uphold the law and protect the prisoner. Just so there's no misunderstanding, I want you to know that I take the resolution to mean that this council's going on record saying that in Lockwood, we're going to have the same law for red men and white men, or black men and green men for that matter. That's why I'm here, gentlemen. If you say otherwise, I'll stick things out till this job's over, but then I'll be moving on."

Eastland turned to Ethan. "What have you got to say about this, Ethan?"

"Will thought he needed a lawyer present," Ethan said, "but I couldn't put it any better than he has. I would like to add something, if I may, though."

"Go ahead."

"Those Indian boys didn't kill the Harpers. I can say that positively. I don't know who did yet. . . . Not for sure. . . . But in just a few days' time, we've come up with a lot of evidence to bring us damn close to an answer. Think about that. Then think about this, too—the men who lynched the Indian boys committed murder just as much as whoever killed the Harper family. I don't think it would hurt to pass the word that anybody who harms Bear Killer is going to be held accountable to the law. . . . I'll see to it. That's a promise."

"You've got two promises on that one," Will Bridges said.

"Now, gentlemen," Ethan continued, "I'm sure you know the

temperament of this town better than I do. Everybody's on edge. There are certain people, some of them well-meaning, a lot of them not, ready to raise hell. And what they call hell is killing Indians. Any Indians. I'm not just shooting at shadows. I passed the saloon before I came over here. I could hear the rumblings. I can't tell you why just yet, but keep an eye on the Circle W riders. They're trying to provide the match to light the fuse, and it won't be that hard to get the job done. I think you could do some good with personal contacts on your own, talking to a few of the fair-minded people, the folks who swing some weight with their common sense. It's amazing what one reasonable voice can do to throw water on something like this. Right now, we just need time. Two or three days maybe, and we'll have some answers that should satisfy folks. But, in the end, that's not important. We either believe in the law or we don't; we can't have it both ways. What kind of a town, what kind of a country do you want to live in? What kind of place do you want your kids to grow up in? That's your choice, and you could be making it by what you do today."

"Ethan," Eastland said, "if you and Will don't mind, I'm going to plagiarize a little and rewrite that editorial of mine. The two of you have said some things that need saying." He turned to the other council members. "What do you have to say, boys? Speak your piece and let's vote."

"I don't know," the undertaker said. "I think we should table this for a day or two and see what happens. Folks will be madder than hell if we make an Indian deputy. I don't think we should go on record yet, not till we know what folks think. We can't do this just for ourselves, you know. We're representatives of the town."

"That's right," Eastland declared. "We're the representatives of the town. They picked us so we could use our judgment on their behalf. Represent. That's the key word. We don't go out and take a poll or get a vote of the people to see if the mayor can go out and take a crap. We've got information they don't have. We have the responsibility to lead; that's part of representing."

"Maybe we ought to see what Gid Webb has to say about this," Caldwell ventured lamely and wiped his forehead which was slick with sweat now.

"Horse shit!" the Journal publisher snapped. "What's he got to do with any of this?"

"Well, he has good judgment about these things," Caldwell responded. "And he has a lot of influence with the people in Lockwood."

"You mean he has a lot of money he spends here."

Ethan had never seen the newspaper editor so feisty.

"I just don't want us to do anything we'll be sorry for," Caldwell whined.

The editor shot Caldwell a scornful look and turned to Dr. Weintraub. "What about you, Henry?"

"There's no doubt in my mind. We have to back the sheriff. We're paying him to uphold the law; we have to give him the tools to do it with. I fail to see why there should be any question of it."

Eastland looked at the German blacksmith whose face was sober and lined with worry. "Do you have anything to say, Herman?"

"Nein. Let us vote. Ich must gehen."

"All right," Eastland declared. "I suggest that this be considered as a single resolution, and I entertain a motion that Red Horse be appointed a lawful deputy to the sheriff of this

Night of the Coyote

town with all the power and authority appertaining thereto, and further, that the sheriff be empowered to deputize such other citizens as may be necessary to uphold the law. Is that good enough, Will?"

"Good enough for me."

Eastland looked at the Council members. "Is there a motion?"

"I so move," said Dr. Weintraub firmly.

"Is there a second? I suppose I could second it myself; I'd rather not." There was silence as all eyes fastened on Herman Roebke. The blacksmith flushed and nodded his head affirmatively.

"Ja. I second."

Ethan looked at Will Bridges and grinned. The sheriff winked in response. They had the vote.

"All right, on the motion," Eastland continued. "Shall this resolution pass? I vote yes. Councilman Weintraub?"

"Yes."

"Councilman Caldwell?"

"No."

"Councilman Roebke?"

"Ja."

"The resolution is passed and adopted," Eastland declared. "I think I can speak for the majority of the Council members; we'll try to talk to some of our friends and neighbors. I'll do what I can with my newspaper, but we can't wait for that. There's work to be done, so let's get at it."

"Thank you, Mayor," the sheriff said. "I'm very grateful for your support."

Ethan was more than grateful. He was proud that he had

picked Lockwood as the place to sink his roots.

18

WHEN ETHAN WALKED through the swinging doors of the Cottonwood Palace, he caught sight of Enos Fletcher hunched over the bar, sucking at a stein of beer, his eyes half-closed and his head bobbing as if he were on the verge of dropping off to sleep. Ethan knew better. The salty old-timer was not missing a thing that was going on in the noisy saloon.

Ethan ambled over to the bar and eased in next to Enos. "Make it a beer," Ethan said, when Max Crabb, the mustachioed, portly proprietor nodded a nervous greeting.

"Don't you think you got enough trouble without lookin' for more?" Enos grumbled without moving a muscle.

"I'm not looking for trouble," Ethan replied. "I'm making a study of my fellow man."

"Ain't nothin' worth studying in the Cottonwood Palace. Anything you'd learn about your fellow man here would be damned disappointing."

"You said I was looking for trouble, Enos. What kind of trouble might I find here?"

Max Crabb slid a beer toward Ethan, and Enos remained

silent until the bartender moved away. "Circle W trouble, and that's the worst kind in Lockwood. If you have eyes in the back of that rocky skull of yours, you'd see there's better than half a dozen Circle W hands swilling booze here this morning. A couple of others come in with them. They got hired gun written all over them. Till you come in, they was gettin' damn loud and big-mouthed about the injun hanging. You wouldn't win no election in this county, Ethan."

"Nope."

"Wouldn't get more than a dozen votes, if that, I'd say. Don't know as I'd vote for you myself. Nothing personal."

"I'm not running for office. I'm representing a client. Tell me, Enos, why do you think the Circle W's so interested in this? Do you have any idea why the Circle W would hire on a bunch of gunslingers all at once?" Ethan asked, baiting the old man.

"Where you been hiding out, Ethan? It don't take no weasel to figure that out. Old Gid's been mad enough to kick his own dog this past year. Rustlers been runnin' off his cows like they had a bill of sale on the whole damn ranch, and he ain't been able to nose up even a hint of who's doin' it. You mean you ain't lost no cows yourself?"

"No, but a herd the size of mine isn't exactly prime for rustling. Stolen cows would be missed too soon. A spread like the Circle W can have cows cut out a few at a time, and it might be weeks before they're missed. In fact, if the rustler doesn't get greedy, the rancher might never catch on."

"Well, Gid caught on to it, all right. Hiring gunslingers ain't his style, but I guess he saw no other way. According to Joe Hollings, he laid out a roll as big as a wagon hub to get these fellars in from Cheyenne. Been here over a month, but story is there ain't been no work for them. Seems the rustlin' stopped soon as they showed up."

"I think they finally found a little work," Ethan said. "But doesn't it strike you strange that this many of Gideon Webb's hands would be in the Cottonwood Palace this time of the day in early June? They're not here because they're short of work. I'm sure there are other ranchers that might see things Gideon Webb's way, but they aren't sending half their crews in to drink away the day."

"Yep, it's strange all right. There's some stranger things goin' on, too."

Ethan waited for the old man to enlighten him, but when Enos did not, he spurred him on. "What kind of 'stranger things' are you talking about?"

"Well, what's Clete Webb doing here, for one thing? Old Gid might be crooked as a snake, but he's got more sense than to send that squirrel-brained whelp in here to do the dirty work."

"Clete's here?"

"Yep, nursin' a bottle over in the corner. The kid's got a temper hot as a branding iron fresh from the fire. This is the last place Gid would want him to be. It's a good bet he's here on his own."

Ethan cast a glance over his shoulder, and his eyes fastened on Clete Webb slouched at a table in a shadowy corner of the room, his own smoldering eyes boring in on Ethan. Clete looked younger than his twenty-two years, Ethan thought. Boyishly handsome, with curly, flaxen-blond hair, he was a heavy-boned man, standing a good six feet four inches, but his bulk had a mushiness about it that confirmed his reputed aversion to hard work and his ruddy face seemed fleshed with baby fat. He had a sullen look and his lips were frozen in a scowl.

Ethan turned back to Enos. "I've got a hunch Mr. Webb is one of those men who turns mean with his liquor."

"Mean enough without it. But you're right, his disposition don't improve none with whiskey in his belly. You know, Ethan, them strange things I was talkin' about . . . there's another thing. Might mean somethin'—might mean nothin'."

"Why don't you just tell me and let me decide."

"Ethan, you recollect telling me to keep my eyes open about the Harper killings?"

"Yes. Did you hear something I should know about?"

"Maybe."

"Well, go on, Enos."

The grizzled man cleared his throat as if he had a bad cold. "I don't know, I think I got me a busted talk box."

Ethan got the hint. "I don't have any cash with me, but if it's good information, it'll be worth two cartwheels next time I stop by."

"Well, now your credit's good with me, Ethan, but I ain't too crazy about waitin' to file a claim against your estate. And the way thing's been around here lately, that prospect's a little more than likely. How's about I stop by your office this afternoon to collect?"

"That would be fine, Enos. Just tell Miss Wyeth I said to pay you. Now, why don't you tell me what I'm getting for my money. I hope it's worth two dollars."

"You know a fellar by the name of Joe Hollings?"

"Joe Hollings . . . ," Ethan thought a minute. "Sure, I remember Joe. Circle W hand. I bailed him out of jail a year or so ago; he'd had too much to drink and got in a fight here at the

Cottonwood. Seemed like a decent sort of guy. I got him off with a fine and sent him on his way with some unsolicited advice. He must have followed it because far as I know he hasn't been in trouble since."

"Not till lately, nohow."

"What do you mean?"

"Old Joe was in here yesterday looking for a job. He was nervous as a hen at a mass meetin' of coyotes. I had him pull up a chair to the table and even put myself out for a drink."

"You're a generous man, Enos, no doubt about it."

"Couldn't begrudge him one. That boy was mighty upset and nobody to talk to . . .'cept me, of course."

"Why?"

"He don't much like what's goin' on out at the Circle W these days. The place is crawlin' with hired gunslingers, he says. Says he'd bet a month's pay somebody done in Grant Richards."

"The Circle W foreman?"

"The same. Grant's just plain disappeared, according to Joe."

"Did he say when?"

"Yep."

"Well?"

"Ain't been seen since the afternoon before the Harpers was killed."

"Did Hollings have any idea about what happened at the Harper place?"

"Nope, but he saw some of it."

"What do you mean?"

"Well, he was with some of the Circle W hands that went over to help put out the fire. You know, he said Clete was the one that drug Cynthia and her daddy out of the house. Guess old

Jake was laying just inside the door and the gal a bit beyond. Clete went just plumb crazy, according to Joe. Howled and bawled over Cynthia like a nursing cow over her dead calf. He said Clete sure as hell had blood in his eyes after that. Joe knew somebody was gonna die before the night was out, just didn't know who."

"Then Joe was in on the lynching?"

"No. Hell, no. Ain't likely that would've happened if Joe'd been there. He's as gritty as eggs rolled in sand, and he'd of stood up to the others. Includin' Clete, if need be. He slipped away though, and skedaddled it back to the Circle W to tell Gid what happened. Till lately, he's always thought the world of old Gid and figured he'd get things in hand."

"What did Gideon say?"

"He wasn't there. Turned out he was someplace playin' poker with some friends, Joe said. Joe decided there wasn't nothin' else he could do, so he just stayed put. When Gid come home later, he was just plain broken up about it all, accordin' to Joe. Next day, when he heard Clete and the Circle W boys was in on the lynchin' of them Indian kids, Gid got madder than a bear with two cubs and sore tits."

"You said Joe thought the world of Gid until lately. What do you mean?"

"It's all over them gunslingers. Joe don't know what's goin' on, but he knows them gunhands report direct to Gid, and it ain't just cattle rustlin' business. Joe thinks maybe Gid is using them to clean up some of Clete's shit."

"I'd like to talk to Joe," Ethan said. "If you see him before I get around to tracking him down, tell him that, would you?"

"Yep, I can sure enough do that. He may be too spooked,

though. He don't want to lose his job till he finds another. He's sparkin' a gal and hopes to marry in the fall."

"Tell Joe I'm in the market for a top hand, too. I'm going to have to find somebody to take Ben's place. Maybe we can strike a bargain that can help both of us. Tell me, Enos, you've been around here longer than I have. Could Grant Richards be mixed up in this?"

"You mean, would Grant have killed Jake and the gal? I'd bet my stable against it. Not unless he had good cause, and there just ain't no good cause for something like that. Besides, I think Grant was sort of sweet on Cynthia Harper."

Ethan's eyes brightened with interest. "How sweet?"

"Well, as far as I know, it was pretty much one-sided, but Grant went callin' to the Harper place on a couple occasions I know of. And when he had to palaver over at the stable, he couldn't help but talk about Miss Cynthia. Wasn't no doubt in my mind but what he was bit good and hard by the love bug. On the other hand, you could say that about a dozen men where Miss Cynthia was concerned. There ain't but three or four gals of ripe marryin' age in the county, and Miss Cynthia was the class of the lot. Damn pretty gal and sharp as a bullwhip's sting. She probably liked Grant well enough, but she weren't ready to settle down by a long shot. She had her pick of the litter, and she was takin' her time choosing."

"Still," Ethan said, "it's a damn strange coincidence."

"I already said that much, law wrangler. Hell, maybe it's nothing. Maybe Grant'll show up here tomorrow. I know this much; it would just about do old Gid in if something happened to Grant or if he took a notion to ride off to lusher ranges—which ain't likely, 'cause Gid always took care of Grant real good."

"What do you mean?"

"Some say he's more son to Gid than Clete is. Joe told me once that if Gid had to choose twixt the two, he wasn't sure who'd come up on top."

"How do Grant and Clete get along?"

"Like two stags fightin' over the same territory. They've hooked antlers plenty."

"Hey, law wrangler," came a slurred, belligerent voice from behind Ethan. "Where's your squaw?"

Enos became a statue at the bar. Ethan stiffened slightly and took his first sip of the warm beer before setting down his mug.

"I'm talking to you, Ramsey. I ain't used to asking questions twice."

This time Ethan turned his head enough to catch a glimpse of Clete Webb who was staggering his way past the table and chairs and moving in on Ethan's right. Ethan turned back to the bar. Clete was a big man, all right. Not more than an inch or two taller than himself, but outweighing him by a good seventy-five pounds. Baby fat or not, Clete Webb had shoulders and biceps like huge hams, big chest, thick and broad like a buffalo bull's. A little soft in the belly maybe, but there was no way Ethan Ramsey was going to lick Clete in a fair fight. And with half the people in the saloon on the Circle W payroll, even if he whipped Clete, the odds were against his walking out on his own two feet. Enos was right—he had shown lousy judgment in stopping at the Cottonwood Palace.

"I'm waiting, Indian lover," Clete snarled, his voice booming in Ethan's ears.

"Any good ideas?" Ethan murmured to Enos who was still

frozen at the bar.

"I don't know you, mister. Never met up with you before in my life."

"That a yellow streak I see running down your back, Ramsey?"

A rough hand closed in a vice-like grip over Ethan's shoulder and spun him around. Ethan saw Clete Webb's cocky, crooked smile for just a second before the young man's face twisted in agony as Ethan's knee drove into his groin like a sledge. Webb doubled up in pain, gasping frantically for breath, as Ethan's fist hammered into the side of his nose. The crunch of bone told him he had broken young Webb's nose.

Taking no chances, he slipped his Peacemaker from its holster, feinted off to one side of the dazed, tottering giant, and slammed the pistol butt against Webb's temple. The blow felled him like a slain bear, and he crumpled in a heap on the barroom floor, lying there in the stunned silence of the room, blood streaming in rivulets down his cheeks and neck, spewing from his shattered nose. It had not been a fair fight.

Ethan spun away and moved for the door, but he was cut off by two Circle W hands who closed in on him menacingly, like wolves stalking an injured calf. Ethan slashed between them, driving his forearm down on the smaller man's neck. The man stumbled away, and, for a moment, Ethan thought he would make it to the door, but the other cowhand, younger and quicker, rammed a fist in the side of his face, dazing him just long enough for the other Circle W hands to swarm upon him like angered bees.

Ethan tried to tear away, taking a blow in the kidney before he rammed his head into the belly of one of his attackers. They punched and kicked and pommeled him nearly senseless, bouncing him from one to the other like a rag doll, and he fought back swinging wildly and missing two blows for every one he struck. Still, two more of the cowhands joined Clete Webb on the floor before someone smashed a table leg across the back of his skull. He reeled and pitched forward, clutching his injured head as he dropped to his knees, struggling to get up. He was only vaguely conscious of the warm sticky blood oozing between his fingers before someone drove a booted foot into his groin.

"Take some of your own medicine, you son-of-a-bitch" he heard someone say. He was devoured by excruciating pain, fighting for breath, as he heaved and wretched, and then a dizzying blackness consumed him, and he collapsed unconscious in his own vomit.

19

ETHAN'S NEXT AWARENESS was of awakening on a narrow cot in an austere and sterile room with gray walls. As his eyes tried to focus, he made out the blurred outlines of the framed certificates on one wall, and he saw the crude wooden surgical table that told him he was in Dr. Henry Weintraub's office. He heard footsteps move across the floor toward the bed, and he winced at a dozen stabs of pain when he tried to shift his weight and turn toward the sound. There were three men, their forms shadowy and ghostlike. As his vision began to clear, he made out Sheriff Will Bridges and Enos Fletcher, and the bushy-browed Dr. Weintraub, the latter whose calm, stoic face inspired confidence, but told Ethan nothing.

"I won't even ask you how you feel," Dr. Weintraub said as he and Sheriff Bridges moved two chairs in next to the bed. "You're going to hurt like blazes for several days. Just answer some questions for me. Are you nauseous?"

"No. My gut hurts like hell, but I'm not sick to my stomach —not now."

"Your vision. You seemed confused when you regained

consciousness. Can you see all right?"

"Now I can. Everything was fuzzy at first. My head feels like a horse stomped on it."

"Table leg," Enos said. He leaned over the table, studying Ethan like a curious cat and scratched his whiskers thoughtfully. "Harley Stafford swung it. Didn't mean nothin' personal, though. But you acted like you was going to whup the lot of them."

"No help from you, that's for damn sure, Enos."

Enos chuckled. "If the Lord intended me to fight like a dog, he'd have given me longer teeth and sharp claws."

"Enos came and got Will and me," Dr. Weintraub said.

"Not while the Circle W crowd was around, I'll bet," Ethan retorted.

"If it helps any," Enos said, "old Clete looked worse than a calf with slobbers when they drug him out of there. You didn't make no friends at the Cottonwood Palace this morning."

Morning. It suddenly occurred to Ethan that he had no idea how long he had been out. "What time is it?" he asked.

The sheriff tugged at the gold chain that was looped on his trousers and pulled out a gold pocket watch. "A mite past five-thirty," he said.

"Five-thirty." Ethan raised himself gingerly, futilely trying to evade the soreness that seemed to be everyplace. "I've got to get back to the ranch. Skye's out there all alone. She'll be worried, and it's not safe for her to be out there."

"You'd better stay here overnight," Dr. Weintraub warned. "You're in no shape to travel. You've had a concussion. These things are unpredictable as the devil, and I don't want you taking any chances. Will can send someone out for Miss dePaul."

"I appreciate your concern, Henry, but I'm going home. I'll

need your services tomorrow, though."

"How's that?"

"I want you to take a look at the remains of Jake and Cynthia Harper. If Will can spare him from the jail tomorrow, I'd like to have Red Horse take us out for a look-see."

"Things seem quiet enough since the Circle W crew rode out. I can get along without Red Horse for awhile. I'd planned to get out there myself, but there's no way me and Red Horse can both stray away from town. And I've had other priorities today."

"It's been almost a week," Dr. Weintraub said. "I don't know how much I can tell. It won't be a pleasant experience, I assure you."

"Nothing about this has been pleasant, Henry, but we've got to find some answers before more innocent people get killed."

Will Bridges and Dr. Weintraub assisted Ethan to his feet and helped him put on his tattered shirt and coat. Enos trailed behind as Ethan limped stiffly toward the door. "I'll saddle up your horse if you can ride, Ethan, or you can use one of my buggies. No charge this time—if you bring it back in the morning."

"I can ride," Ethan said, although the agony in his groin made him less confident than he sounded. Before he went out the door, Ethan turned back to the sheriff. "Will, we haven't had time to really pore over everything that's happened, but doesn't it strike you that the Circle W's activity these past few days goes a long way beyond ordinary Indian hating?"

"I can't deny that, but I can't prove anything criminal yet."

"You know Clete Webb and some Circle W hands were involved in lynching those boys. Have you considered making arrests?"

"By the time they got to Lockwood, there were a dozen people in on that lynching, but they were all spectators," the sheriff said sarcastically. "Nobody will say who did what. The truth is, nobody probably remembers. Folks go loco in a mob. Nobody has a mind of his own at times like that."

"Can the Webbs account for their time that night?"

"You ain't giving me much credit, Ethan. As soon as you told me about the Webb name coming up when you and Miss dePaul were jumped in the mountains, I chased their stories down. Gid's time is pretty well accounted for. He was playing poker over at Charlie Langford's place most of the night. Calm as could be and holding good cards the whole night, Charlie told me."

"I see."

"And three or four Circle W hands will vouch for Clete. They say he rode with them from the home place when they saw the flames at the Harpers."

"What if the hands were in on it?" Ethan asked.

"It's possible, I suppose. But you've got to ask why, and I come up with nothing for motive."

"Killings take place without motives."

"Sometimes. Not often . . . not in these parts. And as for the Webbs' hostility towards Indians, there's something else you might not know. Gid's wife, Clete's mother, was killed and scalped by Sioux not more than ten years ago."

"That could explain it," Ethan said dubiously. "But I'm not buying that notion now. One more thing, Will."

"What's that?"

"When was the last time you saw Grant Richards?"

20

THE RANCH YARD was dark as the inside of a coal mine when Ethan rode in. Churning, ominous thunder clouds blotted out the moon and stars, and the hills that rose above the ranch buildings dropped shadows that crowded out what little light there might have been.

The house was pitch-black. The livestock stirred in the corrals, but there was no sign of human life.

Ethan dismounted and led Patch up to the hitching post in front of the house, his right hand stroking the butt of his pistol as he watched and listened. Where in the hell was Skye? He should not have left her alone. She was too impetuous, too reckless. She didn't appreciate the dangers that lurked in the valley these days. He should have insisted she come to town with him. But he had, he reminded himself, and she had ignored him. He had yet to see her do a damn thing she did not want to do.

He limped into the house, and reluctant to expose himself by lantern light, he checked out the rooms in darkness. Satisfied that Skye was not there, he went back outside and stood on the porch, surveying the corrals and ranch buildings. He checked the horse corrals and was surprised to find Razorback there, for the stallion was far and above Skye's favorite mount.

Then he heard the distinctive whinny of a mare from the barn, and the feeble response of a newborn colt. Skye was probably in the barn playing midwife.

He hurried to the barn and opened the door, picking up an oil lantern and lighting it before moving to the rear where the mare was quartered in the stall. A shiver of excitement raced through him, and for several moments he stared in wonderment at the newborn. The first Appaloosa born on the Lazy R. A beauty, too. A glistening black with white splotches, like patches of fresh mountain snow on the flank and butt. A broad strip of white with little pepper flecks ran the full length of the nose and cut off sharply above the eyes. And a filly, to boot. That's what he needed in these early years—females, future brood mares to build the herd on.

He was so elated with his discovery, that he had forgotten about Skye for an instant. Where was she? She had been there. The bloody feed sacks that were draped over the bucket in the corner of the stall were evidence of that. She must have given the mare some assistance or at least cleaned up the frisky colt. She probably couldn't have resisted it.

He was gripped by near panic. She would have heard him ride in if she had been here. He could not remember the last time he had felt such cold fear. He stood there collecting his thoughts, trying to think like Ethan Ramsey, Army scout, instead of Ethan Ramsey, lawyer.

The barn door creaked, and he whirled in the same instant that his Peacemaker leaped into his hand. But if he had been anyone other than Ethan Ramsey, he would have been too late, for Skye dePaul stood in the open doorway, her eye looking down the sights of the Winchester that was leveled at his chest.

"Skye, for God's sake, put that gun down. It's me."

"Ethan." She paled, lowered the rifle and ran to him. "Ethan, I did not think it was you. I recognized Patch, but you were not wearing your hat and you did not sit right in the saddle. And the way you walked." Her eyes widened in shock when she reached him, and she gasped in horror. "Ethan, my God! What happened? Your face—"

"It's a short story, but let's save it for later." Now the pain that had been stifled by his concern for Skye returned, and his head began to throb violently.

"Where were you?" he asked. "I was worried sick. I couldn't see a sign of you anywhere."

"You were not supposed to. I was out here with the mare when I heard you coming up the road. You should have been back hours ago. I was afraid something had happened to you. I guess it did. Anyway, I hid out in the trees at the far end of the yard. I am sorry; I just did not want to take any chances."

"Don't be sorry, Skye. It's a welcome switch."

Her eyes narrowed, and she looked at him curiously for a moment before she took his hand in hers. "Let us go into the house. You are hurting and you are hungry. Perhaps I can do something about both."

21

NAKED TO HIS waist, Ethan leaned forward on the kitchen table while Skye gently bathed his back with a wet cloth. The cool water soothed his aching ribs, and he began to feel drowsy. Skye was an efficient nurse, and the only thing consistent about her, he thought, was her unpredictability.

The past several hours, she had been a perfect example of domesticity. She had prepared a tasty beef broth and hot coffee that warmed his insides, yet had not forced him to stretch his sore, stiff jaws beyond endurance.

While he was eating, she had disappeared for an hour, returning with a sack full of herbs and plants that she promptly boiled into a pasty concoction she was now proposing to administer to his wounds. He was not about to argue with her; he did not have the strength to resist her. And no man could carry on a debate with a mule.

Without warning, Skye slapped some of her remedy on his pulsating scalp wound. Ethan leaped from his chair, cracking his knee soundly on the table as he got up. "Damn it, woman," he roared, "you're pouring salt on my cut. It burns like hell. It hurts worse now than it did before. I've taken enough punishment for one day."

She planted her hands firmly on her hips and looked at him with disgust, but her gleaming dark eyes betrayed her. She was laughing at him. She placed a firm hand on his shoulder and shoved him back into his chair. "Do not be such a baby," she chided. "This is powerful medicine. It just stings for a moment, then your pain will be gone."

He was not going to admit it, but she was right. The poultice had some kind of numbing effect on the wound. The initial burning had vanished, and now he could almost feel the Sioux medicine shrinking the swelling on his scalp, sucking away the pain. After that, he yielded silently to her treatment, flinching when the paste was applied to open wounds, but uncomplaining nonetheless.

He did not tell her about his bruised and tender groin.

When she was finished, Skye added some logs to the fire, poured herself a cup of coffee, and joined Ethan at the table while he told her about his altercation at the tavern.

She gazed pensively at the steaming tin cup in her hands for some moments before she looked solemnly at Ethan and spoke. "It was a foolish thing to do," she said, "going into the Cottonwood Palace."

He sighed. "Not again. I've already been told that a time or two, and I don't care to discuss it anymore."

Skye shrugged. "Very well. But I want you to know that I do not consider the damages you did to Mr. Crabb's place of business legitimate legal expenses. I will not pay any such costs that appear on my bill."

The woman's tongue was sharper than a well-honed Bowie

knife, and she did not know when to quit cutting. "I had no intention of including the damages on your bill." He pushed his chair back from the table. "Look, I'm tired out. I'm grateful for all you've done, but we can talk in the morning."

He caught a spark of anger in her eyes and saw that her fine jaw was set in that determined way she had. He scooted his chair back to the table. "We'll talk tonight," he said resignedly. "You've got something in your craw; why don't you spit it out?"

She sipped silently at her coffee, staring at the flickering flames in the fireplace, as he studied her, suddenly being much more interested in her physical presence than in what she had to say. He wished she did not have to be so serious, that she would smile more. But even her somberness could not detract from her sleek beauty. Her skin was the color of light polished copper and just as smooth. Her features—her nose and cheekbones and chin —might have been carved and whittled by a master craftsman, yet she seemed oblivious to her splendidness, unaware of the effect she had on him. And surely upon other men.

Or did he see her through clouded eyes? He had an uneasy feeling she was getting some kind of a hold on him that he would have to face up to soon.

He was scrutinizing the firm swell of flesh that rose from above the scooping neckline of her buckskin shirt when she jolted him back from his musings. "I would like to know what your plans are," she said.

He looked up and saw the reprimand in her eyes.

"I presume you are already formulating some strategy. I certainly did not employ you for your dubious skills as a fighter."

He sloughed off her jabbing remarks. "Yes, I have some ideas. I've already told you, though. I'm riding out to the Harper place with Henry Weintraub in the morning. There's a chance we can turn up some evidence that will exonerate Bear Killer and his friends."

"It will be too late to help Screeching Hawk and Raven Eyes, and it will not keep white idiots from lynching Bear Killer. Why are not the men in custody who murdered those boys?"

"Skye, you're being unreasonable. It was too late for Screeching Hawk and Raven Eyes when you came to me, and Will Bridges and other good men are prepared to protect Bear Killer—with their own lives, if need be. I understand your frustration. I share it. Often, the law moves too slowly . . . sometimes unfairly. But it's all we've got. Without it, we're just a bunch of animals trying to kill and feast before we're killed and feasted upon. The law is the only hope we've got for people to occupy the same space without stomping all over each other. You believe that, too, or you wouldn't have come to me in the first place. Maybe the law isn't the only problem; maybe you need another lawyer."

Skye was silent, and it was only then, when he saw the tears glistening in her eyes, that Ethan realized how deeply troubled she was.

"Skye, it's not my handling of the case that's bothering you; it's something else. What is it?"

She bit her lower lip, straightening before she spoke. "There is nothing bothering me, Ethan Ramsey, that cannot be resolved by you doing your job and ending my need for your legal services as quickly as possible."

He reached out and took her hand in his. "I don't believe you," he said softly. She tried to pull away, but he gripped her hand and got up from his chair, pulling her up to him. Again, she tried to slip away from him, but his arms closed around her.

"Ethan," she protested, struggling against his unyielding arms. "No, don't—"

His lips sought hers. She tried to evade his kiss at first, but when their lips touched, Ethan found no resistance, only soft, moist eagerness. Her fingers began to gently rake his back and her body relaxed and became pliant, molding to his own. He released his hold on her and began to stroke her back and firm round hips, but she did not break away. His quick, frantic breathing was matched by her own, and he knew that her willing body was ravaged by the same fire that consumed his own. He wanted her as he had never wanted any woman. ·

His hands slipped beneath her shirt, working upward and slipping over the taut flesh that sheathed her ribs, before coming to rest on her breasts. Suddenly, she flung herself back as if he had stabbed her with a knife. He moved to take her back into his embrace when her hand shot out, whacking him sharply across his mouth, opening the cut on his lips. He backed off and saw the panicked, petrified little girl before him, her eyes wide as a frightened doe's. Her face was a mask of terror.

"Skye, damn it. It's all right. I wouldn't hurt you. What's the matter with you? I thought—"

She shook her head repeatedly as if denying something to herself. "This cannot be, Ethan," she said, her voice husky. "This cannot be." She backed away from him.

"Skye, I'm sorry. I lost my head. Sit down with me at the table; we'll talk. Calmly and sensibly."

"No, I cannot talk right now." Tears began to stream from her eyes and race down her cheeks. Then she turned away and rushed off to her bedroom.

Ethan felt utterly defeated when he sunk in to the feather bed on the cot near the fireplace. He could hear Skye's uncontrollable sobbing in the next room, and he was torn by the urge to go to her, comfort her. It was a rarity—a lawyer at a loss for words. He did not know how to deal with Skye dePaul. At this moment, he did not know how to deal with himself.

Mercifully, sleep took him quickly.

Ethan slept several hours past sunrise. When he got up, his head was groggy, and there was some stiffness in his chest and shoulders, but he did not feel all that bad considering the beating he had taken. He gave credit to Skye's Sioux liniment for that.

He observed that the fire was crackling in the fireplace, and that the coffee pot was brewing on some coals near the edge. Skye was obviously up, but he had not even heard her activity in the room. He could have sworn he felt her soft lips touch his gently as he slept. Perhaps it had not been a dream after all.

On the table, Ethan found a jar with a chunk of comb honey in it and a loaf of bread Skye had apparently baked the day before. He also found a note. As he would have expected, her handwriting was clear and steady and fine.

Ethan: I will be staying in the dormitory at the Pennock School. I hope you do not object to my borrowing Razorback until the case is settled. I do wish to have you continue to act as my lawyer. I apologize if I implied otherwise. Skye.

It was the kind of note you might expect from Skye. Cool, terse, to the point, yet mysterious and distant. For the sake of his own sanity, he had to get this case concluded and chase this crazy woman out of his head once and for all.

22

IT WAS A half hour before Ethan had to meet Dr. Weintraub and Red Horse at the sheriff's office, so he decided to stop at his own office and check with Katherine Wyeth. A look of horror formed on his secretary's face when he walked in the door, and he realized that his bruised and swollen face must be nearly unrecognizable.

"It looks worse than it hurts," Ethan said.

She got up from her chair. "I should hope so, or I don't think you'd be able to walk into the office on your own accord. The story's all over town. It must have been terrible."

"Not a very good way to drum up business, is it Katherine?"

She smiled uncertainly. "I would have said so a week ago, but already this morning I have made two appointments for you for next week. Ray Stearns wants you to make a new will for him, and Clem Dawson wants you to handle the purchase of a small ranch he's planning to add to his holdings. Mr. Dawson said he didn't know if he agreed with what you were trying to do, but—these are his words, not mine—'Ramsey's got more guts than you can hang on a fence.'" She smiled.

"I wonder if I'll ever see the day when I'm hired for having a good legal mind. I guess I'll just have to tell myself they want the right lawyer for the wrong reasons." Then he turned serious. "Why don't you sit down, Katherine? I'd like your help on something."

He let himself down into a chair in the reception area opposite Miss Wyeth's desk. "I'd like to know a few more things about Gideon Webb," he said. "I don't like to keep putting you in this uncomfortable position."

"I'm uneasy talking about Gideon, but I can't imagine anything you would ask that would have to do with our . . . our personal relationship. So why don't you just tell me what you need to know? I'll help if I can."

"Either the Circle W is trying to stir up an Indian War, or somebody out there doesn't want the truth to come out about the Harper killings. Has Gideon Webb ever said anything to you that would point to his involvement?"

"No. Gideon's wife was killed by the Sioux, of course, but I never noticed that he was especially bitter about it. He rarely spoke of her death. If he did, it was in the way one might speak of a loved one who died of smallpox or cholera. Besides, an Indian uprising wouldn't be good for business for the Circle W, and with Gideon, business always comes first. Always," she added meaningfully.

"How did Webb and Jake Harper get along? Webb built an empire gobbling up small ranches, and according to the county plat map, the Circle W adjoins the Harper place on three sides."

"What you say is true," Miss Wyeth agreed. "He's bought up ranches after the owners went broke, but there's never been a hint of violence surrounding his land acquisitions. He's always used his money for leverage. And Gideon always spoke very highly of Jake Harper. In fact, Jake was usually hired on by the Circle W during roundup. If Gideon had wanted to squeeze Jake out, he certainly wouldn't have been helping him earn extra money. I know it sounds like I'm being defensive about Gideon, but I'm trying to appraise him honestly. He's arrogant and vain, ruthless where business is concerned, but I think he's also basically law-abiding. I recall him saying one time 'violence breeds violence.'"

"You told me before that Gideon was building everything for his son, and that Clete's been his greatest disappointment. Would Gideon kill to protect his own son?"

Her brow wrinkled, and she sat silently for some moments before she replied. "I don't know. I truly don't . . . but he might."

"What about Clete?" Ethan asked. He touched his swollen face gingerly. "I know about his temper. Is he an Indian hater?"

"Oh, yes," she said. "I'm sure he would be an Indian hater, but I doubt if it's an obsessed kind of hate. He hates most white people, too. He is a very angry, hostile young man."

"Would that have included the Harpers?"

A look of astonishment crossed Miss Wyeth's face. "Oh, no. My goodness, no. Jake Harper was one of the few men who could get along with Clete. I suspect that was one reason Gideon liked Jake so much."

"And the girl, Cynthia?"

"Clete was crazy about Cynthia. Of course, so were half the young men in the county."

"Was he seeing her?"

"Yes, but he hadn't spoken for her or anything like that."

"How did Gideon feel about Clete's interest in Cynthia?"

"Oh, he approved . . . totally. He thought marriage might

settle Clete down. We didn't talk about it all that much, but I'm certain he encouraged the match."

"How did Cynthia feel about this?"

"I don't know that she reciprocated Clete's affection, but I never heard anything to indicate she disliked him, either. She danced with all the men at the barn dances. She had a naturally pleasant and outgoing disposition. I had the feeling she liked a lot of young men and wasn't ready to fall in love yet."

"I have to head over to the sheriff's office, but there's someone else I want to ask you about first. Grant Richards."

"Grant Richards?"

"Yes. I've heard he's quite close to Gideon."

"More than close. He's the son Clete was supposed to be. Sometimes, I think Gideon would be better off if Grant moved on because Grant's a constant reminder of everything Clete can't live up to. I'm sure Grant's closeness to Gideon isn't easy for Clete, either."

"Did Gideon ever say anything about a rivalry between Grant and Clete?"

"Not that I recollect. He did mention once that he wished they could be better friends. I think he hoped that some of Grant would rub off on Clete."

"Have you heard anything about Grant Richards being absent from the Circle W since the time the Harpers were killed?"

Her eyes widened in surprise. "Why, no, but I haven't talked to Gideon or anyone else from the Circle W since that noon after Miss dePaul came into the office. I don't think Gideon's been to town since, so for all I know he could be missing, too. I truly don't know what else I could tell you. Gideon and I rarely confided in each other. You might say we were just mutual antidotes for loneliness."

"Katherine, one more thing. You evidently find Gideon attractive. What is it about him that interests you?"

"His manners, for one. He doesn't talk a great deal about his background, but I know he is from the East. He mentioned once he'd spent some time in Boston. He's not the typical rancher I've encountered here. If you'll forgive me, Mr. Ramsey, I must say that many of the men here are coarse, if not downright uncouth. I've never heard Gideon use profanity. Oh, I'm certain he does on occasion but never in the presence of a lady. He dresses impeccably, always the perfectly tailored, vested suit. He's very well read and shares books from his library with me on occasion."

"I hate to ask you this, Katherine, but did Gideon see any other women?"

She shrugged. "I don't know. He's been calling on me for several years. Sometimes, I'd see him as often as two or three times a week. Then I might not see him for several months. Until the day Miss dePaul came into the office, I had not seen Gideon for nearly three months. If he was seeing someone else, he was being very discreet about it. Of course, discretion is Gideon's nature. But I doubt if that was the case. It was roundup time, you see, and he would have found it difficult to get away from the ranch. I saw little of him the previous spring as well."

23

THE THICK OAK door of the limestone sheriff's office was barred when Ethan arrived. He rapped on the door.

"Who is it?" called Will Bridges.

"Ethan Ramsey."

The sheriff opened the door and Ethan stepped into the office. He spotted Dr. Weintraub sipping at a cup of coffee at the sheriff's desk. Red Horse stood near the window with a shotgun cradled in his arms.

"Sorry to keep you waiting, gentlemen," he apologized.

"Frankly, Ethan," Weintraub said, "I'm surprised you made it in this morning. There's no medical logic for your being able to crawl out of bed after the beating you took yesterday."

"I had a good doctor." He didn't have the heart to tell Henry about Skye's doctoring. He turned to Will Bridges. "Will, nobody seems to know a whole lot about Jake Harper and his family. What can you tell me about them?"

"Not a hell of a lot, either. Jake kept pretty much to himself. Gid Webb's the only man in these parts that I know of that got on with Jake. It wasn't that he was a mean cuss or anything like that."

"How long had they lived here?"

"Oh, about four or five years. His missus died about a year after they settled here giving birth to a boy child. The baby passed on a month later. I only saw his woman once. Grey-haired, kind of sickly looking. Past child bearing prime by quite a ways." He shrugged. "She shouldn't have got with child again, but there's lots of women on Boot Hill you can say that about. What do you do? People being people, having their natural urges?"

"The girl, Cynthia . . . she was more outgoing, I'm told."

"Oh, yeah, that's right enough. All the young bucks knew Cynthia and were crazy about her."

"What about their finances? I understand Harper worked some for the Circle W during roundup to make ends meet. He must not have been too well off. Does that jibe with what you know?"

"Don't know nothing for a fact, but Jake had kind of a puny spread. It ain't likely he could have eked out much of a living there. Besides, except for Gid, all the ranchers around here are land and cow poor. Or ain't you noticed?"

"I've noticed. I fit in fine on that count. Will, are you on good terms with the Lockwood State Bank?"

"Good enough. I've done a few favors for Clyde Van Sykes. I got a chit or two I could call in if that's what you're getting at."

"You can learn a hell of a lot about a man," Ethan said, "by the way he handles his money. I don't mean whether he's poor or not, I'm talking about where it comes from, who he pays it out to. Show me a man's financial transactions for a year, and I can write you a story about his life. Since Jake Harper's dead, and there aren't any known relatives around to object, I wonder if you couldn't persuade Van Sykes to work up a list of Harper's financial dealings with his bank for the past few years. If he won't go through the trouble, get permission for me to go into the bank and review the records with him. Charley Langdon's the bank's lawyer, and I'm not sure I'd get much help on my own."

"Clyde's kind of a stuffy old turd, but I don't see why he wouldn't cooperate," the sheriff said. He smoothed his bushy mustache and nodded his head. "Yep, I guarantee he'll help us out. I'll see him first thing this afternoon."

"Thanks, Will. Now, if it's all right with you, I'd like to step back and talk to Bear Killer a minute before we ride out."

"Go right ahead. I ought to call this visitors' day at the jail."

"What do you mean?"

"Oh, I thought you knew. Miss dePaul was in to see him a few hours ago. Enos is in with him now."

"Enos? What kind of business would he have with Bear Killer?"

"Poker business. He's teaching the kid to play cards. And from the moaning and cussing that's coming up here, I'd guess it's like teaching a man to use the gun he's going to shoot you with. I had to pay the old fart double wages to sit in for Red Horse while he's out with you. The town board ain't gonna like it, are they, Doc? They think Enos is always gouging them for something."

"I don't think that judgment is unfair, Will," the doctor replied, "but I'll back you up on it. The old coot has a certain honor—if he takes your dollar, he'll do exactly what he says he's going to do for it. Of course, he'll try to figure out a way to milk out another dollar after the job's done." He brushed his hand through his wiry black hair. "You know, Enos Fletcher lives like a pauper, but when he dies, perhaps I should say 'if,' I think we're going to learn that he's the richest man in the county. I know he exchanges all of his paper money for gold and silver coins. If he hasn't figured out how to take it with him, it'll be like digging for buried treasure after he's gone."

Ethan excused himself, and left the others to conjecture about the enterprising ways of Enos Fletcher. Closing the door that separated the sheriff's office from the chamber of jail cells, he joined Enos and Bear Killer who sat on a bunk in the open cell and were so absorbed in their card game, they were unaware of Ethan's presence. Ethan watched as Bear Killer spread out four aces on the blanket.

Enos threw his cards down and spat a slimy wad of tobacco on the jail floor. "Damn you, boy, you're crooked as a snake in a cactus patch. There ain't no way you could hold them kind of cards."

Bear Killer grinned wickedly. If they didn't get him out of here soon, Ethan thought, he was going to take a lot of unwelcome white culture back to his village.

Ethan interrupted. "Enos, I'd like to talk with Bear Killer a minute."

The old-timer jerked his head around. "Why, good morning, Ethan. You look so purty this morning, I almost feel like takin' my hat off to you."

The livery man gathered up his cards and got up from the bunk. He nodded towards Bear Killer. "Watch the cub, here, Ethan. I think he aims to get his folks' land back by playin' poker. Goddamn, I feel like I turned against my own kind teachin' him the game." He let fly with another tobacco wad that splattered between Ethan's feet and removed some gooey remnants from his beard with a swipe of his arm and hobbled out the door.

Ethan sat down next to Bear Killer. "So now you've met Enos," he said. "What do you think of him?"

"He has the manner of a bear waking from his winter's sleep. But in his heart, I think he flies with eagles. I like him." The boy drew his legs up in front of him and clasped his hands about his knees. "What brings my friend, the Puma, to this place?"

"Did the sheriff tell you that Charlie Carlson confirmed your story about being at his place the day the Harpers were murdered?"

"No, he did not. Did you not believe what I told you?"

"Yes, I believed you, Bear Killer, but like it or not, we needed to be certain a white witness would back you up."

"You did not come here to tell me this."

"No," Ethan said, "I wanted to ask you about something Charlie told the sheriff. Charlie said you left his place about seven o'clock. Is that right?"

"I would not know. I can read a white man's clock, but it means little to me. I know that the sun was just beginning to fall behind the mountains when we left."

"That would be about right. Why didn't you stay over? That seems like an odd time to leave, especially when some of your people are kind of spooky about roaming after dark."

"Brule do not fear the darkness. Not the warriors among us. But we waited until night because we believed we could ride unseen until we reached the mountains of the Brule. We thought it would be safe. We were wrong."

"But you didn't go more than five miles, and you stopped right in the middle of ranch country. Why?"

"Screeching Hawk's pony became lame. It did not seem

serious, and we thought if he rested the night, the pony could travel by morning, and Screeching Hawk could change off riding double with Raven Eyes and me. Our foolishness was in building a fire."

"How long were you at your camping place before the riders came?" Ethan asked.

"I cannot say in white man's time." He thought a moment. "As long as it would have taken to ride back to Mr. Carlson's and return again."

"You were riding slowly?"

"Yes, there was no hurry."

Two or three hours would have passed from the time the Indian youths left the Carlsons to the time they were captured, Ethan thought. That meant the evening was still young when Jake and Cynthia Harper were killed.

"My cousin says she will find the true killers," Bear Killer said.

"Your cousin? Skye?"

"Sky-in-the-Morning is unhappy with you. She told me she would go to the Harper ranch and learn for herself what happened that night."

The woman was more than he could cope with. If she would just sit still a few days, maybe he could get to the bottom of this.

"Why is she unhappy with me? Did she say?"

"She gave many reasons, but she did not give the real one."

"And what is that?"

"It is not for me to say. The coyote is guiding you both. It would be bad medicine for me to interfere."

24

THE THREE RIDERS skirted the silent ranch yard that was deserted except for the charred remains of the home and outbuildings that had once been the hub of lives and living. Red Horse edged his bay mare into the lead as they swung away from the Harper ranch, climbing into the aspen-cloaked foothills to the west.

Ethan looked back over his shoulder, struck suddenly by a great sense of sadness as he watched the ruins fade behind him. He could never get over the fragility of human life. A man has plans and dreams. He goes through each day working for tomorrow when he will take time to sit back and watch the sunset or when he will find someone to share his life with. What are the chances of reaching tomorrow? Jake and Cynthia Harper never would. In brief moments, their lives had been snuffed out and everything tangible they had built had gone up in flames and vanished into the wind.

Like himself, Jake and Cynthia Harper had no known family. Unless a will turned up, the disposition of Jake's small landholdings was in doubt. A hundred years from now, who would know they had ever walked this earth? There was no immortality of this world. Perhaps that was why so many men placed their bets on heaven; it was intolerable to them to accept the notion of nothingness after life. It was a sobering thought.

"You're quiet, Ethan. Do you feel all right?" It was Dr. Weintraub, who bounced uncomfortably on a sway-backed gelding at Ethan's side.

"I'm fine, Henry. Just daydreaming."

"About the lovely Miss dePaul?"

"No, that hellcat just shows up in my nightmares."

"For a lawyer, you're not a very good liar, Ethan. Just how much farther do we have to go? I'm not accustomed to this kind of riding. I'm going to have more bruises on my butt than you've got on your face."

"You'll be a better doctor for it, Henry. You'll have more compassion for your patients' suffering."

Ahead of them, the Pawnee reined in his horse and dismounted. Moments later, Red Horse led them to an outcropping of rock jutting over a shallow ravine, at the bottom of which was a huge mound of caved-off shale. The Indian got down on his knees and began to scoop the rock away with his hands. Ethan and Dr. Weintraub joined him with shovels, and by the time the scorching sun said it was high noon, they had uncovered the blanket-shrouded bodies of Jake and Cynthia Harper.

Ethan and Red Horse dislodged the bodies and carried them up the slope and placed them in a shaded glen off the trail, while Dr. Weintraub retrieved his bag. When the doctor returned, he let loose a deep sigh and knelt down and began to unwrap the larger of the bodies. The decaying, grotesque corpse he uncovered gave off a putrid odor that turned Ethan's stomach. A body five days dead was not a pleasant sight, but Ethan had expected to find worse.

So, apparently, had Dr. Weintraub. He pulled away the blanket that shrouded Cynthia Harper. Not even Cynthia could be beautiful in death, Ethan thought, recalling the several occasions he had seen her flitting gaily past the merchandise in the Lockwood General Store.

"I thought they were pulled from the fire," Dr. Weintraub said. "I don't see any burns on these bodies. They certainly didn't die by fire."

He plucked a kit of scalpels of various shapes and sizes from his bag and commenced his grisly chore, noting his observations in a professorial monotone as he worked. "No mutilation; they were not scalped. Mr. Harper was shot in the chest, apparently twice. I should be able to find the bullets."

Ethan noted that Red Horse, who had spoken barely a word the entire journey was totally absorbed in the process, squatting on his haunches, his neck craned over Harper's bloated corpse. Ethan turned away and strolled off to the edge of the clearing to seek some fresh air. This was Henry Weintraub's domain, and the young doctor was welcome to it.

Ethan sat down and leaned back against the trunk of a ponderosa and waited. He was about to doze off when Dr. Weintraub called to him.

"Ethan? I've got some answers for you now."

Ethan got up and rejoined Weintraub and Red Horse. Dr. Weintraub handed him a crusty chunk of lead. "The remnants of one bullet passed through his right lung and exited through the interior of the scapula, the shoulder blade. This one appears to have deflected off a rib and pierced the aorta before it lodged between the third and fourth thoracic vertebrae."

"Talkin' like damn foreigner," Red Horse said. "I seen whole damn thing. Something to see, by damn."

"He didn't suffer," Weintraub said. "I don't know a great deal about firearms, Ethan, just enough to repair the damage they do . . . if the victim's lucky. Do you have any idea what kind of gun might have fired it?"

"I think it might be a Smith & Wesson .44—the new Russian model. Wouldn't be more than half a dozen of the guns in the county. It's not a weapon a Sioux Indian boy would be using, that's for damn sure."

"I wish I could tell you more, Ethan. There's a whole new science developing on these things in the East. Terribly fascinating. Mark my word, someday they'll be able to recreate the whole scene of a crime from autopsies. They won't just be identifying the caliber and kind of guns used; they'll be matching the bullet to a specific weapon. Of course, there's no way we can do that now."

"Not precisely," Ethan said, "but we can sure narrow down the possibilities." He was suddenly exhilarated by the progress they had made. "And what about Cynthia? Did you find any bullets?"

"No, she wasn't shot."

Ethan's brow furrowed. "Then what?"

"The flesh about her throat was bruised. Her trachea was crushed. She died from suffocation but not because of smoke inhalation."

"Strangled," Ethan said, his voice a near whisper. "Was she violated?"

"I couldn't say, not after this much time. But there's something else; I don't know what to make of it."

"Henry, you have a bad habit of keeping a man in suspense."

"She was pregnant, Ethan. The young lady was carrying a two or three month old fetus in her womb."

"I don't believe it."

"I'll show you if you like."

Ethan backed off, waving the doctor away. "That won't be necessary, Henry. It's just that this was the last thing I expected. It raises all kinds of questions, and I don't even know what they are. I'll say this, we've learned plenty this morning. You're a genius, Henry. I just wonder if your Harvard education isn't going to waste out here in the West."

"Is life less precious out here?" Dr. Weintraub asked.

His question did not require an answer.

25

IT WAS MID-afternoon by the time they finished burying Jake and Cynthia Harper in the Bar H family plot that was also the last resting place for Jake's wife and infant son. The last chapter of the Harper family history, Ethan thought. There had been a lot of last chapters written in the settlement of the West, and there would be many more before the story was finally told.

Dr. Weintraub, his role in their mission concluded, had returned to Lockwood alone, leaving Ethan and Red Horse to bury the dead. Ethan turned to the venerable Pawnee now. "Well, friend, what do you say we take another look-see around this place before we head back to town?"

The sober-faced Indian nodded agreement, and the two men walked slowly down the hillside that sloped away from the tiny graveyard. Ethan and Red Horse searched the rectangular building site, working their way from opposite ends toward the debris that was framed by the foundations of the former ranch structures.

As they neared the remains of the house, Ethan's trained eyes picked up fresh signs. Tracks. Horse and human. "Red Horse," he called as he squatted down and bent over the tracks. They were clean and distinctly formed in the fine dust, not yet feathered out by the wind as the other shallow, fading prints were. He looked up at Red Horse, whose intense, scrutinizing eyes belied his stoic face. "This morning, don't you think?" Ethan asked.

"Yep. Damn Sioux moccasins."

"Only one pair though," Ethan said. "Someone not too heavy. Small print. A woman."

"Damn big horse," the Indian said.

"Skye and Razorback."

The Pawnee began combing the area like a bird dog trying to pick up a scent, while Ethan followed the incoming tracks to the limestone foundation of the house. He saw where Skye had evidently tied the horse to a fallen timber and ferreted out her moccasin prints in the ashes of the home where she had apparently made a search. Out of curiosity, he followed her course.

"Left in damn big hurry," Red Horse remarked as he worked his way back toward Ethan.

"Maybe she found something."

"Maybe. Or maybe damn scared. Tracks point to mountains. Maybe warrior lady goes to see damn Sioux brothers."

Warrior lady. Red Horse had just paid Skye as great a compliment as he was probably capable of giving a woman. Ethan continued to work his way through the rubble. He tripped on a splintered, fallen timber and pitched forward before he caught his balance on another. That's when he saw it. The charred, naked, human skull lying in a pocket formed by the crisscrossed roof timbers that had caved in during the fire and formed a mausoleum-like cavern for the poor soul who lay beneath.

"Red Horse," Ethan said, the words almost choking in his throat. He could tell that Skye had seen it, too, for some of the debris had been cleared away. Pushing away the half-burned timbers that blocked his way, Ethan crawled in for a closer look.

Red Horse silently slipped in beside him. The skull lay near the edge of a scattering of bones, parts of which were chalky white. Ethan surmised this was where turkey vultures and other scavengers had stripped the residue of flesh from the bones.

Ethan picked up the skull and examined it. It's size and length and the thickness of the leg and arm bones left no doubt that the body was that of a man. He was interested in a ragged hole at the rear and top of the skull. He handed it to Red Horse who gave it a quick scrutinizing and placed it in the nest of bones.

"Bullet hole?" Ethan asked.

"Maybe. Could be damn fire."

"I think the rest of the skull would have been burned worse," Ethan said. Henry would probably know.

"Maybe."

Ethan stood up and scanned the ruins. He nodded toward the far end. "The fireplace was over there. From the break in foundation, I'd say the door was on the south wall."

Red Horse got down on his hands and knees and began sifting through the cinders near the skeletal remains. Momentarily, he fished out a curved object that had the appearance of a charred fragment of china, and passed it to Ethan who evaluated it, running his fingers along its rough edges. "Porcelain," Ethan said. "From the shape, I'd say it was part of a chamber pot, and as long as I'm guessing, I'd say this man died in a bedroom. I wish Henry hadn't gone back to town. We have some more work for him."

"Too damn much work," Red Horse said.

"I won't argue that. Anyway, we can't leave this poor devil's bones here. I'll get my poncho out of the saddlebags and wrap the remains in it. You can ride back to town with them and let Will Bridges and Doc Weintraub ponder this a spell."

"Spirits madder than damn hell if can't find damn bones. Don't like this."

"The quicker you get back to town, the sooner you'll be rid of the bones," Ethan said. "So let's get to work and get your package wrapped."

"You want me to take damn bones alone? What you gonna do?"

"I'm going to try and pick up Skye's trail. I've been thinking about it. . . . If she rode into the mountains, she was either looking for something or running from something. Either one could spell trouble."

26

WHO WAS THE third victim? Why hadn't the Harpers' bodies perished in the fire along with the unidentified man? Could the man have killed the Harpers and been slain by Jake as his last, dying act? It was conceivable, but remotely so. Who would have set the fire then?

Ethan considered the possibility that the bones were those of the missing Grant Richards. But that didn't explain a thing.

He slowed Patch. A short distance ahead, another trail, a deer or cow path, forked into the wider one he followed. He reined the horse to a halt and dismounted as he approached the juncture. The broken brush and the track-blotting hoof prints there told him that others besides Skye now rode ahead on the trail. As many as five riders, shod horses. He knew now why Skye had taken off from the Harper ranch in such a hurry. She was running from someone.

As he forged ahead, he observed that one of Skye's pursuers had dropped off the trail and was obviously trying to cut off Skye's escape. Any lingering doubt that the men were stalking her was removed.

Icy fear chilled his spine. They had three, perhaps four hours head start on him. His chances of closing the gap in time to help Skye were slim to none. His best hope was that she could somehow elude them. Sundown was less than an hour away and darkness should work to her advantage. The mountains were her domain. That would give her an edge.

As he broke around a sharp turn in the trail, his hopes were dashed by the dead horse that blocked his passage. Razorback. The magnificent, unruly stallion that had shown respect for only one. Tears stung his eyes as he swung down from the saddle. He had cried for more horses than men in his lifetime.

Quickly, he scouted the area, putting together a sketchy story of what had happened there. Razorback had taken a bullet in the neck, and evidently floundered helplessly for some time before death ended his suffering. The bullet had struck him from the left side, so it was likely fired from higher up the mountain. That meant the rider had been successful in his effort to encircle Skye.

She had escaped for the moment, however. It appeared she had either leaped from the horse, or had been thrown free when the animal went down. Ethan picked up her trail easily enough. Wisely, she was angling toward steep, rocky mountain slopes that horses would not be able to take. If they were going to track her down, they would have to abandon their horses.

But she was not armed. Her Winchester was still in its saddle holster, pinned under the fallen horse. She would not have been able to yank it free without a struggle, and that would have made her an easy target for the bushwhacker.

Ethan knelt down by the dead horse and worked the rifle free. He then retrieved his saddlebags and his own Winchester and removed Patch's bit and bridle, deciding the Appaloosa would be harder to capture and hold that way. Yet, if he did not fall into the wrong hands, the empty saddle would signal that the rider was in trouble.

Ethan rubbed the horse gently on his velvety muzzle. "Good boy, Patch. Run like hell, fella." He pointed the horse back down the trail and slapped him sharply on the rump. "Go home, Patch. Git."

The horse lurched forward, stopped and looked back at Ethan. Ethan ran up to him and slapped him again. "Go home, boy." Then as the horse headed down the trail, Ethan disappeared into the thick aspen.

They wouldn't catch him easily, Ethan thought as he listened to the rhythmic gait of the powerful gelding. Patch was getting older, but he was a one-man horse, and had been chased more than once under circumstances like these. The first whiff of anything human, and the horse would take off like an explosion from hell. Any other horse burdened with a rider would have a tough time making a close race of it.

Ethan looked to the north, the direction Skye was headed. He could make out the faint gray outline of Scalped Ridge in the distance. The slate-colored highland that formed a rim around a narrow grass-carpeted valley rose higher than any other rock formation in the vicinity and appeared to be skinned naked along the top where salty alkali deposits discouraged even the most hardy vegetation. Hence its name—Scalped Ridge.

If Skye knew the ridge area, she would head for it, for on the steep slopes and cliffs below its crown were numerous caves and recesses that offered shelter and hiding places.

It was an hour's walk as the eagle flies—a good four scrambling up and down the rugged slopes and rocky escarpments that blocked his way. And he had to be wary of the unknown enemy that was stalking Skye.

Night's blackness would drop in the mountains soon and cover Skye's trail like a dark blanket. This fazed him not at all. Many whites knew the Sioux called him Puma; few were aware he had been so named because he preferred to move and attack at night, like his namesake, searching out and destroying his prey from the shadowy chasms of darkness.

27

ETHAN THREADED HIS way through the maze of brush and aspen and ponderosa, trading haste for silence. He had been on the move for several hours without picking up any sign of Skye or her pursuers. She was covering her trail well. He was still guessing that she was working toward Scalped Ridge, but for all he knew she could have doubled back or been pressed to another course.

The night air was damp and bone-chilling. The low growl of thunder in the west portended a storm before morning. He wished now he had not surrendered his poncho to Red Horse. Clad only in buckskin shirt and denim trousers, he was not dressed for a night in rain-soaked mountains. And to light a fire was to invite death.

No sooner had the thought passed through his mind, than he saw a sudden flash of light in a dense growth of trees not more than fifty feet ahead of him up the slope. He froze in his tracks, standing there for several minutes while he searched for the source. Then he caught movement in the trees: the arc of a man's arm swinging upward, the gray outline of the wide-brimmed hat pulled low over his forehead. He was leaning against a tree, dragging lazily on a cigarette, indulging a habit the would shortly cost him his life. A hefty man. A fool.

The question was not whether to kill, but how. He would have to do it quietly. Ethan lay down his saddlebags and the two rifles, and his fingers closed on the cold bone handle of his Bowie knife. The gunman was looking for a woman. All of the men on this mountainside were his compadres.

Ethan started walking up the slope, noisily crunching the sticks and pebbles beneath his feet, brushing his shoulders against the low-hanging limbs. The man gave a start at the sound of Ethan's approach and moved away from the tree. When he caught sight of Ethan, he walked toward him without hesitation, his rifle nestled casually in the crook of his arm. "Race," he drawled, "is that you? Did you find that red bitch?"

Ethan did not reply, but walked steadily toward him. He was within twenty feet of the scraggly-bearded man before he was recognized. Ethan saw the man's eyes widen in shock, and at the same moment, his bulky form froze. He fumbled to position his rifle as he croaked, "You're not Race. Who are—" Before he could get off a shot, Ethan's arm whipped back and his wrist snapped, releasing the missile in his hand with slingshot-like quickness. The long keen blade that buried itself to the hilt in the man's throat cut off his life almost as quickly as it had cut off his words.

Ethan pulled out the knife and wiped it clean on the dead man's trousers. Then he retrieved his rifles and saddlebags and slipped into the dense growth where he had first sighted his victim. To wait and listen.

As he stood there in the protective shadows, he appraised the situation. In a few minutes time, he had learned several things of considerable interest to him. Race Sanchez was one of the riders who had followed Skye. Her would-be killers had elected to scatter out—a sound strategy if you were chasing an unarmed woman. More risky if, in a sudden turnabout, you became the pursued. Most important, Skye was still alive—at least the last the dead man knew.

A silent, webbed bolt of lightning illuminated the sky; the rumble of thunder, sounding like the unrelenting fire of army canons moved nearer. Suddenly, an eerie calm descended upon the mountains. Not a bird called in the night. Not even the aspen whispered.

It was then that he heard it. Something, or someone, breathing. They were labored, rasping breaths, yet so light that at first he thought his ears were deceiving him. His hand inched toward his pistol and slipped it from its holster. He shifted into a crouch and spun around to face nothing but a seemingly empty forest.

He stood there, motionless as a marble statue, poised to fire. Then he heard it again from a tangle of gooseberry bushes off to his right, not more than thirty feet away. He leveled his Peacemaker at the brush and spoke evenly and softly. "I hear you there in the brush. My gun's aimed right at you. Come on out with your hands raised high."

No one emerged, but he got a reply. "Ethan? It cannot be," Skye's voice choked.

He lowered his gun and raced to the brush. Oblivious to the stinging barbs that scratched his hands, he parted the brambles and found her in a nest-like pocket in the midst of the dense undergrowth, curled up on the ground, one arm jammed tight against her abdomen. A wave of nausea swept through his gut, leaving him weak. Holstering his pistol, he forced his way through the brush and moved to her side.

"What is it?" he asked. "Are you hurt?"

She looked up at him, and even in the darkness, he could see that her eyes were glazed with pain.

"Ethan, it really is you. I am not dreaming." Her voice was feeble and strained.

"Skye, are you hit?"

"It is my arm," she said. "When Razorback went down, I was thrown. I do not remember how it happened." She clenched her teeth and could not keep the tears from squeezing out of the corners of her eyes. "It is very bad," she said, "very bad."

"You'll be all right. I'll see what I can do now; then we'll get out of here."

Gingerly, he traced his fingers the length of her left arm, searching, probing. Skye gasped as he pressed the flesh midway between her wrist and elbow. Momentarily, he discovered why. Not only was the arm swollen and distended, but a shard of bone protruded like splintered wood through the flesh. The darkness hid some of the ghastliness of it, but he did not need a surgeon's lantern to know that Skye was right. It was very bad.

Her forearm was caked with sticky, half-dried blood. She had obviously bled profusely for a time. "The bleeding," he said. "How did you stop it?"

"A wild grape vine; it is tied about my arm."

He located the crude tourniquet nearly hidden by the puffy flesh that ballooned beneath it. He admired her resourcefulness and was in awe of her calm demeanor. "How long has that been tied there?"

"Shortly after I was thrown. Every time I loosened it, it

began to bleed again."

He tried not to betray his anxiety. "I'll release it now. Maybe you've got it stopped." He carefully untied the cord-like tourniquet and waited. Blood oozed from the wound, but it appeared to be only a trickle. "I think we can get along without the tourniquet," he said, "but I can't set the bone. Not here, anyway. I'm going to see if I can splint it well enough to move you. There's going to be a hell of a storm, and it could hit anytime. Our best bet is to head for Scalped Ridge and find shelter in one of the caves there. We can build a fire and see what else can be done about that arm. Are you strong enough to walk?"

"I was trying to reach Scalped Ridge, but the bleeding had sapped too much of my strength. I grew weak and could go no further, so I found this place and prayed. My prayers were answered."

"Which God did you pray to?" Ethan asked, trying to gauge her sense of humor. The perfect whiteness of her weak smile brightened him in spite of their dilemma.

"Both of them," she said. "The white Quaker God and the Great Spirit. I did not wish to take any chances. If you know of any others I might pray to, please tell me. I fear we shall need all of the gods in every heaven and happy hunting ground before this night is done."

He placed his hand on Skye's forehead. She was burning up. "With all due respect to your gods, Skye, I think we're going to have to help ourselves out of this one. The first thing we'd better do is to get that arm wrapped. I'll be back in a minute."

He returned soon with several ponderosa branches and a belt, shirt and pair of trousers he had stripped from the dead man. He knelt down beside Skye and warned her. "I'm going to help you turn over on your back. I'll be as gentle as I can, but it's going to hurt like hell."

"You do not have to swear, Ethan. I understand what must be done. And do not worry, I shall not cry out. I do not wish for our enemies to find us. Please talk with me when you bind my arm. . . . It will help."

Carefully, slowly, he helped her roll over onto her back, and then he worked the flannel shirt around her forearm, wrapping it tight to cushion and steady the protruding bone.

"The man I killed," he said, as he continued working on her arm, "was not more than thirty feet from this spot when I first saw him. It's a miracle he didn't find you here."

"He had not been here long," she said, her voice quavering. "These men are not trackers or they would have found me long ago. It was an accident he was near this place. But very fortunate for me, as it turned out. Several of the men passed by me shortly before sundown. They, of course, would have deduced where I was going. I suspect they finally realized what may have happened and sent one or more of the men back. This man appeared very nervous. I could hear him pacing. He may have been lost. Most men, white or Indian, are cowards in the darkness. It is unlikely they are searching for me now, especially with the storm moving in."

"Yes, I think you're right. They'll be trying to get back to their horses and find a place to hole up. Odds are they'll wait till morning to take up the hunt. They'll figure you won't go far on foot. Do you think they know you're hurt?"

"It is likely. I fell against a tree after Razorback was shot. I was stunned for at least several minutes, and then I crawled away into the trees. The gunman would have seen that."

"Why were they after you?" Ethan asked.

"One cannot be certain, but I believe it may be because of something I said to Mr. Webb."

"Webb? What do you mean? Which Webb?"

"Gideon Webb."

He had never heard her speak so meekly. "What were you doing talking to Gideon Webb? And where?"

"I went to see him at the Circle W."

"That was a damn stupid thing to do," he said, forgetting the gravity of her condition. "Why, on God's earth, would you go to see Gideon Webb?"

"I found something in the ashes of the Harper house."

"You mean the bones."

"That, too. But this was something I was certain belonged to the Webbs, presumably Clete Webb."

"What was it?"

"A gold pocket watch . . . a very expensive one, I would judge. It was somewhat charred and tarnished, but the Circle W brand was engraved on the case."

"That doesn't explain why you went to Webb's. Why didn't you just bring the watch back to town?"

She hesitated then looked up at him sheepishly. "I . . . I was angry with you, Ethan . . . or I thought so at the time. I suspect I was more angry at myself for being such a child. Anyway, impulsively, I decided to confront Mr. Webb with the watch. I had heard such good things about him. Even you had told me that he had a reputation for being an honorable man. I thought if I confronted him with evidence that his son was implicated in the killings, he would see that nothing could be served by further bloodshed."

Ethan was incredulous. "You gave Gideon Webb the watch?"

"Oh, no, I did not do that. I hid it between loose foundation stones at the southwest corner of the Harper house. I simply told Mr. Webb that I had found such a watch, and that it was evidence to be used against his son."

"What did he say?"

"He appeared very calm about it all. He expressed surprise and insisted there had to be some other explanation and stated he knew nothing about any gunmen. I was certain he was lying; still, I found him very much a gentleman. In fact, if I may say so, there is a quality about him, a strength, that I found quite magnetic, almost seductive. I must admit that Gideon Webb is the kind of man a woman would like to believe."

"But you didn't?"

"No, I did not. Several times, he asked me to produce the watch, and his interest was more than casual. I could tell it was causing him some dismay. It is not so difficult to understand that a man might resort to drastic measures to save his own flesh and blood. I do not excuse him for it; I simply understand."

"Did he make any threats?"

"Never. He just said he would give due consideration to my information and would make a decision soon. He suggested I turn the evidence over to the sheriff. That is precisely what I intended to do when I left the Circle W. I returned to the Harper ranch to pick up the watch, and I had just started to get it from its hiding place, when I heard horses. So, I left the watch where it was and rode away. I thought I would return, but, of course, they did not give me the opportunity."

Her breathing was deep and rapid, and he could sense the

tension in her body. The pain that racked her had to be close to unbearable.

Cutting some strips from the legs of the scavenged trousers, Ethan secured the sticks about the padded arm and used the remnants of the trousers to make more cushioning and to fashion a crude sling. He used the belt to bind Skye's upper arm tightly to her body. When he was finished, the arm was as nearly immovable as he could make it. Unfortunately, he thought, that did not overcome the terrible truth that he had been unable to set the bone. He would try that later.

But the more he learned of her injury, the more grave his doubts about his ability to help her.

Now he assisted her to a sitting position and sat down beside her, wrapping his arms about her shoulders and supporting her there, giving her time to shake off some of the dizziness he knew she would be feeling from the loss of blood and hours of lying on the ground.

Suddenly, as if it had been waiting for Ethan to complete his task, the wind wailed like a howling wolf through the trees, and a scattering of heavy raindrops burst from the Skye. "How do you feel now?" Ethan asked.

"Better. I can walk. We must go."

"The pain?"

"It is not so bad now."

She was lying; he could hear it in her weak, trembling voice. He could feel it in her taut, shivering body. Never had he wanted so much to share someone's burden, to carry all of someone else's agony. It was a strange feeling for one who had walked most of life's trail alone.

He did not have time to ponder. With good luck, it was an

hour to reach any haven on Scalped Ridge, and he had no reason to expect good luck.

He helped Skye get to her feet. She was wobbly as the newborn colt she had helped deliver the night before. He did not even try to argue with her. He knew she would walk until she fell. After that, he would do what he had to do.

28

IT HAD TAKEN several hours for Ethan and Skye to accomplish the grueling trek up the narrow deer trails that ended at Scalped Ridge. Rain had exploded from the sky, spilling to the earth in sheets and torrents that had made the climb slippery and treacherous. Skye had fainted dead away no more than a half hour after they embarked. Ethan had scooped her into his arms, abandoning one of the rifles, balancing the other precariously across Skye's hips as he trudged through the storm.

Finding a cave had been the easiest part, and now, as the flames of the fire he had lit began to bite at the wood and send forth the sweet fragrance of pine smoke, Ethan surveyed the cave. It was no more than seven or eight feet deep, perhaps five feet at its highest point, with a ceiling that tapered to an opening of less than three feet.

The entrance was half hidden by an outcropping of rock, forming a crude portico that helped keep the cave bone dry. Beneath the cave was a steep shale-covered incline that dropped off some fifteen feet to the deer trail Ethan had traveled the last stretch of their journey. The cave fortress would be nearly impenetrable from attack, but they could not withstand a siege of any duration. Food was nonexistent. With his hands, he had dug four small pits on the loose rock outside the cave, forming small cisterns to collect rain water. He hoped that the rock beneath was not too porous to retain water.

Shortly, he would shape a crude cup from a chunk of cedar. In any case, the water supply was scant and could be cut off by any attackers.

The worst of it was that Skye's condition left them with no time.

As the damp wood dried and the hot breath of the fire began to warm the cave, Ethan took another look at Skye. She stirred restlessly now. Her unconscious state, he surmised, was the result of weakness and exhaustion and pain, not the effects of the simmering fever that was only beginning to gnaw at her. The fever would do its damage later with the inevitable infection that would threaten both limb and life. Her entire body shook spasmodically, but he, too, felt like he had just emerged from a mountain river in January.

He pulled off her moccasins and peeled off her rain soaked breeches and shirt and stretched them over logs to dry before he took off his own and did the same.

He lay down next to Skye, giving the warmth of his body to her backside as she slumbered facing the fire, knowing that false modesty or any imagined impropriety were foolish when their survival was at stake.

In spite of his determination to keep a vigil, he too surrendered to sleep. He awoke when the fire died down, and after building it up again checked their garments to find they were fairly dry. He got dressed and made a clumsy attempt to get

Skye into her trousers, when her eyes opened.

"Ethan?"

"It's all right, Skye, you're safe. I was drying out your clothes."

She was struggling like a turtle on its back, trying to get up, and he moved to help her. She appeared somewhat rested and stronger, but he knew her improvement was temporary, for when his hands touched her bare flesh, it was like holding them over hot coals.

"It's easier to take off another's clothes, than to put them back on, is it not, Ethan?"

Her mind was working. She was not delirious—yet. "I won't argue that. If you'll help me, maybe together we can get you dressed."

He helped her worm into the trousers and her tattered shirt. Some women, he thought, would be horrified at the notion of being undressed in their sleep under such circumstances. Skye seemed unembarrassed by her naked state, accepting his actions as he had intended them, as a sensible approach to solving an immediate problem. The Sioux in her perhaps? Indians did not seem to share the white man's uneasiness about unclothed bodies. Many white people were afraid of their bodies, and they hid that fear behind something they tried to call morality. But the naked body had nothing to do with morality.

"You're thirsty," he said.

"Yes."

He made five trips outside to the water cisterns to fill the hollowed-out wooden cup before Skye waved it away. He drank the last one himself and then moved in next to the fire a few feet away from Skye.

"The wind's died down," he remarked. "It's still raining, but it has slowed some. It should clear off not too long after daylight. I'll see what we can do about clearing out of here then."

"The men will be looking for me, Ethan. Perhaps for both of us if they found the man you killed. We have no horses. You cannot carry me all the way to Lockwood."

"I've thought about that. I won't wait for them to come to me. . . . I'll stalk them. We'll take their horses. We can make Lockwood by early afternoon. I'll get you to Henry Weintraub." He sucked in his breath. "Skye, I don't think I can set that arm. I'd need another man to help. Even then—"

"I know you cannot, Ethan." Her voice was soft and steady. She appeared strangely serene. "I told you before, it is very bad. I have seen such things—and it is unrealistic to think that we will make it to Lockwood by this afternoon."

"We can, and we will."

She smiled benignly and reached up and caressed his cheek with her fingers. "You are a brave man, Ethan Ramsey. A strong man. Yet there is a gentle side to you that I regret I have not yet learned to know." She withdrew her hand and gazed pensively into the fire. "I wonder what might have happened with us? Perhaps it is better that I shall never know."

"Skye, damn it! What in the hell are you talking about? You sound like—"

"Please, Ethan, do not swear. It is very unbecoming. You are an educated man and should be able to choose suitable words to express yourself."

"Then quit talking like that."

"Ethan, I am going to die. It is out of our hands."

"Skye, that's nonsense. And it is not out of our hands."

"Do you believe in heaven, Ethan?"

He could see the pain in her eyes, but otherwise she seemed unperturbed. This conversation she persisted in upset him. But she was facing death. She was entitled to talk about it, even though he was determined not to let her die.

"I don't know if I believe in heaven," he said honestly. "I don't believe in hell, not in the fire and brimstone sense. If there's an afterlife, it's probably nothing like the preachers describe it. But it warms me to think my soul might meet up again with old Ben Dobbs and a few others I've cared about on this earth."

"I have decided to go to the happy hunting ground with my people." Skye said. "I shall call upon the Great Spirit of the Sioux in my last hours. I am closer to their God. If you do not care for the heaven of the white people, Ethan, you may come to see me in the happy hunting ground."

Her eyes held his in the shimmering light, and he saw a sadness and longing that overwhelmed him. "I'll plan on meeting you there someday. But your Great Spirit is going to have to wait a long time before either of us shows up."

"Ethan, you are a very stubborn man."

"You used to be pretty damn stubborn yourself. It's not like you to give up so easily."

"Ethan, would you mind holding me?"

He moved next to her, put his arms about her and let her lie back against his chest. He raked his fingers through her long, sable hair, thinking how beautiful it was, even damp and tangled.

"Ethan, I do not know if I shall pay your fee," she murmured.

He shook his head in disbelief. "The last thing I'm concerned about is my fee, Skye."

"You must think about your fee, because I have employed

you . . . and you have not been doing your job."

"Haven't been doing my job? What do you think I'm doing here?"

"I have wondered about that. How is it that you found me?"

"Red Horse and I went out to the Harper place and picked up your trail there. We could tell you left in a hurry."

"Did you tell me earlier that you had found the remains?"

"Yes. We learned some other things, too." He told her about Dr. Weintraub's autopsy on the Harper bodies.

"I apologize, Ethan," she said after he had finished. "You have been working. The body at the Harper house, do you think he was Grant Richards?"

"Possibly. Very likely, if he's truly missing. Not that it explains anything. You realize that Gideon Webb must have sent those gunslingers after you?"

"Yes, it appears I was foolish to go to him. When I heard the riders coming to the Harper ranch, it was from the direction of the Circle W. The men, no doubt, saw me riding away from the Harpers'. They did not follow me immediately, though. I waited in the trees a quarter of a mile above the ranch and watched. They scattered out and seemed to be searching for something—I suppose they were looking for the watch. I do not think they found it. When they broke away from the Harper ranch, there was no doubt they had decided to come after me."

Her voice began to drag like a person talking in her sleep as she related the story. "There was no way I could get past the men and make it to Lockwood. I decided to seek refuge in the mountains with my people."

Her head dropped against her chest. "Ethan," she said, her voice trailing away, "when I die, take me into my mountains. Do not place me under a cold mound where I will be caged by earth and gobbled up by worms. Bury me in the way of the Sioux on a platform close to the sky, near Waconda. And free. Promise me."

"I promise. But you are not going to die."

She did not respond, and his body went numb with sudden, cold fear. He released a sigh of relief when he felt the rise and fall of her labored breathing. She had drifted off to sleep or into unconsciousness. Whichever it was, he would not disturb it for it was the only anesthesia for her pain.

He lay her down next to the fire and worked his saddle bags under her head for a pillow. He tossed the last of the firewood on the fire and bent over and kissed her softly on the lips. "You won't die," he said. "I won't let you."

He peered outside the entrance of the cave. Sunrise was an hour away. His best chance was to escape into the darkness. In the unlikely event Skye awoke, Ethan left his makeshift cup full of water at her side. Next to the cup, he placed his loaded Peacemaker, on the outside chance she could use it for her protection if things did not work out. He tried not to think about the other use she might have for it.

He took one last look at her, trying to indelibly imprint her face on his mind, and then he turned away, snatched up his Winchester, and disappeared through the mouth of the cave.

29

FROM HIS PERCH on top of Scalped Ridge, Ethan had an eagle's view of the valley below, the spiny ridge, and the pine-covered slopes that afforded the only approach. Since the first fingers of sunlight crawled over the mountaintop, he had been watching the men inch their way toward the ridge, zigzagging through the trees, searching as they climbed. He had the horses spotted, too. They were staked out in a draw near the spot, where earlier, telltale black smoke produced from wet firewood had curled skyward and marked the place where Skye's pursuers had spent the night.

Horses. No more than a half hour away. A downhill walk. Four men stood between him and those horses—between Skye and a doctor. From his position in the rocks, he could hold off four men for a long time. But Skye did not have a long time.

The gunmen had spread out and were well protected by trees and brush. With his rifle, he could pick off one easily enough. But that would warn the others, and they could keep him pinned down, perhaps circle around the rocks, and eventually overrun his position. Odds were, though, it would be a standoff. That was not good enough.

Abruptly, one of the men broke out ahead of the others and made a beeline for Ethan's nest of rocks. He had not been sighted or the gunman would not have been approaching with such abandon. The man, like Ethan, had evidently singled out the best watchtower on the ridge.

Ethan burrowed down in the rocks, watching as the man climbed over the rise and bore in on his hiding place. Damn. All of the choices had been made for him. The gunman carried his Winchester hanging low on his hip. He was a young man in his early twenties, Ethan judged. Fine-boned and swarthy. He was finally going to meet the elusive Race Sanchez.

Ethan waited a moment longer. Then, when Sanchez was within twenty feet, Ethan poked the barrel of his Winchester between some boulders. "Don't make a move for your gun, mister. My rifle's aimed right at your belly button."

Sanchez froze and his reptilian eyes darted nervously. "What the hell?"

"Do as I say, Sanchez, or you're buzzard meat."

"I ain't arguin' mister, but who the hell are you? I ain't looking to do you no harm."

"My name's Ramsey. Does that have a familiar ring?"

"The law wrangler?"

Ethan remained hidden, hoping that the other gunmen would not be alerted to what was taking place on the ridge. "I'll be asking the questions. Did you find your friend?" Sanchez had regained his composure and now appeared quite calm and relaxed. That was when a man of his breed was most dangerous.

"What friend?"

"The friend you're missing. There were five of you."

"So, you're the hombre that done Buster in. I couldn't figure that out. Couldn't see how the woman could have killed him. Last I seen of her she looked to be in damn poor shape."

Ethan's finger tightened on the trigger. "You're the one that shot her horse?"

"I won't deny it."

"Who are you working for, Sanchez?"

"How'd you know my name?"

"Who are you working for?"

"I don't see what I got to gain by telling."

"Your life. We'll bargain—your life for information."

"I don't got you pegged as a killer, Ramsey." He tossed down his rifle; it would be a clear signal to the others that something out of the ordinary was going on. "I don't think you're the kind of man who'd kill another in cold blood."

"Not unless I'm driven to it, and I just have been. Right to the brink." Ethan caught a barely perceptible swaying of Sanchez's right hand that betrayed his intention. "I warned you once. I can see you, but you can't see me. You'll be dead before you slap leather."

Sanchez smiled broadly, revealing white, even teeth. "I got no ideas amigo. You want to bargain? I'm listening. What are you dealing?"

"I told you . . . your life for information."

"You'll let me go free? Just walk away from here?"

"No. I'll take you in, but I won't kill you."

"You're just giving me a choice as to how I die."

"Not if you haven't killed anyone."

"You want to know who I'm working for?"

"You hear right."

"I don't see that it matters none if I tell you. No matter what happens betwixt you and me." The cocky smile seemed to be engraved in his face. "I work for Webb."

"There are two Webbs."

"Not that sniveling pup that calls himself a Webb, that's for damn sure."

"You were hired by Gideon Webb?"

"I ain't going to say it twice."

"Did you kill my partner, Ben Dobbs?"

"Never heard of no Ben Dobbs."

Possible, Ethan thought. Race Sanchez was likely unconcerned with the names of the men he killed.

"What do you know about the Harpers?"

"Burned out by injuns, they say."

"What were you doing at the Harper place yesterday?"

"Just looking around."

"What were you looking for?"

"I'm done answering questions."

"Why did you try to kill Miss dePaul?"

Sanchez's thin lips curved into a scowl. He was through talking, Ethan decided. That suited him.

From behind the rocks, he could not see the other gunmen, and for all he knew, they could be closing in on him. Ethan stood up keeping his rifle fixed on Sanchez's belly. The other men were out of sight. That worried him.

"Throw your pistol down, Sanchez. Take the butt between your fingers and drop it to the ground."

"You're asking me to strip myself naked."

"Do it," Ethan commanded. "Now."

Sanchez's lithe body seemed to coil like a wire spring as he went into a crouch, and his lightning quick hand closed on the six-gun. Ethan's gun cracked twice before the gunman's pistol cleared the holster, driving two bullets into his chest just inches apart.

Sanchez groaned, looked down at his bleeding chest in disbelief and then back at Ethan with astonished eyes. He staggered several feet toward Ethan, still groping frantically for his pistol, before he pitched forward and landed face down on the rocky ground.

A rifle fired from down the slope to Ethan's left and another fired from the right, spraying shards of rock only a few feet from Ethan's hip before he dove for cover. Two of them had him hemmed in, and somewhere there was a third. He doubted that getting Sanchez out of the way had been worth the price of letting the others out of his sight.

He rose up from behind the rock, fired two quick shots and ducked just before the gunmen answered him with shots that chipped more stone. These were not ordinary cowhands, Ethan concluded. They knew their business. What bothered him most was that there still seemed to be only two riflemen. One, he guessed, was in the timber at the fringe of the bald ridge, perhaps fifty yards away. The other must have found a fortress of his own in the rocks off to the right along the spine of the ridge.

If the third gunman had slipped over the ridge during the showdown with Sanchez, he would be hidden from view. He could only hope that the third man had not grabbed the opportunity.

For the better part of an hour, Ethan traded shots with the gunmen. He had their positions isolated now, but he had not drawn blood and did not delude himself that he had much prospect of doing so.

If something did not break his way soon, he decided he would try to charge the gunman in the rocks and hopefully draw him out, or get a better angle on him before he took a bullet. A reckless thought, but he had no better one.

Ethan fired off a quick shot at the gunman in the trees. This time he got no response from either quarter. A few moments later, he fired at the rifleman in the rocks. Again, no retort. He leaned back against a boulder and pondered his dilemma, pulling the brim of his hat forward to ward off the blistering rays of the sun.

His throat and lips were parched and dry. The cave would be chilly, but Skye, if she were awake, would be welcoming the coolness by this time. A gunshot reverberated from the canyon side of the ridge. The cave!

He grasped the rifle and leaped up and raced along the spine of the ridge, disbelieving that he had not been shredded by the gunmen's bullets before he escaped through a break in the rocks that led to the honeycomb of caves. He slid down the slope like a log in a sluice, nearly overshooting his objective and catapulting over the edge of the canyon wall before he dug his booted heels into the shale and clay and tumbled to a stop. He clambered along the slope and saw the body sprawled outside the cave before he reached the entrance. The third man, he guessed, as he barely hesitated, giving the man whose nose had been nearly blown off, only a quick glance before he scrambled through the narrow opening. "Skye, it's Ethan," he called. "I'm coming in. Don't shoot."

Somehow, she had raised herself to a sitting position and was leaning against the rear cave wall, facing the entrance, her good arm propped on one knee, the pistol clenched in her hand and aimed at the cave opening.

"Did I kill him?" she asked as he pried her fingers loose from the gun.

"Yes."

"I am glad. That is a wicked thing to say, is it not? Do you suppose it is the savage in me?"

"Probably." After holstering the pistol, he felt her forehead. It was like her skin was stretched over hot coals. He checked what was visible of her left arm. The flesh was scarlet and puffy. But it was bloated more than swollen. Nearly twice its normal size. The skin had turned dark purple.

"Did you hear the coyote, Ethan?"

He looked into her lifeless, glassy eyes. "Coyote? What do you mean?"

"The coyote was howling. You did not hear it? That is what awakened me. That is when I heard the man outside the cave."

There had been no coyotes howling in the vicinity of Scalped Ridge this morning, but you didn't argue with anyone this sick.

"Did I kill the man, Ethan?" she asked for the second time.

"Yes, I guarantee it."

"I am glad, did I tell you that?"

"Yes, you told me."

"The coyote warned me, Ethan. He told me what to do. I think he was the same coyote Lame Buffalo heard. Is that possible?"

He humored her. "Yes, I suppose so." She was delirious. What reserves she had drawn on to ward off the would-be killer, he would never know. Her eyes fluttered and then closed.

"Ethan," she said sleepily, in a near whisper.

"What is it, Skye?"

"I want to live. I do not want to die." Her head slumped forward, and mercifully, she was unconscious again.

He had to get her to the horses. He was helpless to do anything for her here. Better for them both to die quickly in a rain of gunfire, than to cower in a cave and to watch this woman who had somehow touched his heart, slide inch by inch into the black chasm that was death.

Minutes later, Ethan carried Skye over the crown of the ridge. The men who met him there were not the ones he had expected. Badger Claw, Skye's thwarted suitor, and two other Sioux warriors stood beside the bodies of two white men whose backs were decorated with Sioux arrows.

Badger Claw, his face grim, approached Ethan warily, his brooding eyes scrutinizing the woman in Ethan's arms. He placed a hand on Skye's face and touched her swollen hand and then stepped back and glared at Ethan challengingly. He spoke in Brule Sioux. "We will take her to our village. Our medicine man will say prayers for her, make powerful medicine."

Ethan shook his head. "No."

"We can take her from you."

"No." He had not used his crude Sioux since leaving Fort Laramie, and he answered awkwardly. "You can take her only if you kill me first."

"That would be easy," Badger Claw spat. "We have already killed two white eyes. A third would give us each a scalp." He smiled coldly. "The Puma's scalp would be a fine prize in the village of my people. I would claim it for my own."

"Do you think Lame Buffalo would honor the warrior who killed the Puma under whose protection he placed his own son?

And what becomes of Bear Killer if the Puma is killed by Sioux? Do you wish to answer your chief for that?"

The smile faded from the Indian's face. "Sky-in-the-Morning will die."

Ethan's eyes blazed and locked with those of the belligerent Sioux. "Sky-in-the-Morning will not die. I will not let her die. I must take her to the medicine man of my people. He is a great and wise man. Go to your village and ask your medicine man to chant for Sky-in-the-Morning. Together, the powers of our medicine men can save her life."

Skye moaned. "Ethan?"

"I'm here, Skye. Everything's all right. I'm taking you to Dr. Weintraub now."

"The coyote told me to kill the man, Ethan. I did kill him, did I not?" Her voice trailed off.

When Ethan looked up, he saw Badger Claw was watching her, and he thought he saw a softening in the Indian's stern face. Perhaps Skye was something other than a prospective second wife for him to possess.

Again, speaking in Sioux, Ethan said, "I am going to where the bad white eyes left their horses. Kill me if you must, but if you wish to help Sky-in-the-Morning, you can build a travois to carry her on and provide me water for our journey." He turned away and started walking in the direction of the horses.

30

ETHAN SAT SLUMPED in a chair in Dr. Weintraub's cramped reception room, gazing dreamily at the fluttering flame in the oil lamp that provided feeble light for the room. Dr. Weintraub had relegated him to the chair over Ethan's vigorous protests, insisting he and his nurse would perform their tasks better without an observer in the surgery.

"You don't want to be responsible for our doing anything less than our best, do you?" the doctor had countered. "If you care about her, let us do our work."

The young doctor had won out, and now Ethan was well into his fourth hour of waiting.

They had been escorted to the outskirts of Lockwood by Badger Claw and the two warriors. Shortly before sundown, he had ridden down Lockwood's main street leading the horse that pulled the two-poled travois on which Skye was secured. The town had been quiet when he rode in, but word traveled fast and by the time he reached Dr. Weintraub's office, the street was lined with buzzing spectators.

Will Bridges had been in to express his concern. "We've got

a lot to talk about," Will had said meaningfully. But at the time, it had passed Ethan by. His mind was occupied by one thought —Skye had to live. The feeling he had at the mere notion of her dying could be described in one word—emptiness.

The door to Dr. Weintraub's surgery opened, and the lanky doctor entered the waiting room. Ethan rose to meet him, but Dr. Weintraub waved him back into the chair; he could feel his heart pounding in his chest. "Damn it, Henry, don't do this to me."

"She's alive, Ethan."

He was flooded by an initial wave of relief, but then his apprehension surged. "That's not telling me a damn thing. She was alive when I brought her here. Will she be all right? Will she be alive tomorrow? I want to know."

"I wish I could say. She's a strong one. I think she can survive the infection, but she's in a state of deep shock. These things are very unpredictable. But I'm very hopeful."

"Can I see her?"

"Shortly . . . if you want. But even if she pulls through, it will be several days before she knows anyone. I'll be keeping her sedated with laudanum and some new opiates we're trying."

Weintraub was normally a very easy-going, soft-spoken gentleman who inspired confidence, but Ethan noticed he was fidgeting in his chair, trying to avert Ethan's gaze.

"You haven't told me everything, Henry, have you?"

The doctor sighed deeply and looked up. "I wonder if I'll ever get hardened to these things. Being the conveyer of bad news is the worst part of being a physician." He sucked in his breath. "I had to take her arm, Ethan."

Ethan sank back in the chair. It was like being kicked in the belly by a horse, yet he should not have been surprised. He had seen countless wounds and injuries. Intellectually, he knew from the first moment how it would be. But emotionally, he had denied it.

A suffocating silence filled the room for some moments before Ethan finally spoke. "How much did you have to take?"

"I left about four inches below the elbow. If I could have seen her right away, I might have been able to set the bone. But it was becoming gangrenous. Even then, I don't know. The bone was splintered and twisted badly." He shook his head in defeat. "It's very tragic. She's such a lovely young woman."

"Are you suggesting she'll be less than beautiful because of this?" Ethan replied testily.

"Ethan, don't pick a fight with me. I'm your friend. Miss dePaul's doctor. Of course, I'm not suggesting that. I don't feel that way. But some men might have their fool notions about what a perfect young woman should be, and that might include having five fingers at the end of each of two full arms. There are some who might be repelled by a disfigurement like Miss dePaul's. The important thing will be how she feels about herself. I am not a physician of wide experience, Ethan, but I know how a person can be crippled more emotionally than physically by something like this. You seem to be . . . well, close to her. You need to be aware of this. She may need a lot of support from her friends to make adjustments."

"She'll adjust," Ethan said, "or more likely, she'll make everyone adjust to her. She's one hell of a women, Henry. You could take both arms, and she'd still be the most beautiful woman in Wyoming. That wild, indomitable spirit of hers. Her keen intelligence. Her way of looking at life. They're just as much a part of her beauty—more so, maybe—than all of the fine physical qualities she's blessed with. And she's tough as nails, Henry. She won't quit. She won't die."

Ethan caught the bemused smile that crossed Dr. Weintraub's lips. "Have you admitted it to yourself yet, Ethan?"

"Admitted what?"

"That you are in love with Skye dePaul?"

31

"Enos," Ethan said, "how many men in this county would own a Russian model Smith & Wesson?"

"Hell, how should I know? I ain't no gunsmith. I don't keep no count of what kind of sidearms these jaspers carry around here."

"But you know some men who own Russian models?"

"You just never quit asking questions, do you, law wrangler? Still paying for answers?"

Ethan sighed. "If that's what it takes."

Enos swiped a dribble of tobacco off his cracked lips with his forearm and squinted his right eye. "Five names come to mind. I can give you five names for a dollar."

"Put it on my bill, Enos."

"Well, there's Horace Allgood out at the Diamond A, Clem Wilkins is another. And Bart Lewis. Then there's Grant Richards and Clete Webb."

"Richards and Webb both have Russian models?"

"Gid got a matched pair out of the first issue—gave one to Grant and one to Clete. Joe Hollings said Clete whined for a week afterwards. Thought he should have had the pair."

32

WILL BRIDGES TUGGED at his frosty-gray mustache as he leaned forward on his desk. "You look a little more respectable this morning, Ethan," he said. "Did you get any shuteye last night?"

"Some. A shave and bath helped most, but, yes, I got a few hours sleep. Henry put me up in one of his hospital rooms—that's what he calls them. Near as I can tell, they're just spare bedrooms."

"I guess a hospital's anyplace a sawbones works," the sheriff said. "You know we're going to have to do better by Doc. He's getting quite a reputation. Wouldn't it be something if this town could have an honest-to-God hospital?"

"That's a good thought, Will."

"How's Miss dePaul this morning?"

"Henry's quite optimistic now. She's gained consciousness, but he has to keep her so doped up no one can carry on a conversation with her. She knew me ,though, when I stepped in to see her."

"Did Doc Weintraub tell you about the bones you sent back with Red Horse?" Will Bridges asked.

"I didn't even think to ask. I had too many other things on my mind, I guess. What about them?"

"Doc thinks the poor devil was shot. He was hard put to think of anything else that would have made a hole like that in the fellar's skull."

"I thought as much."

"There was something else. Doc said the man had a broken leg once—left leg, above the ankle."

"A lot of men have had broken legs," Ethan replied.

"Yep . . . including Grant Richards. Left leg above the ankle . . . about three years ago, I recollect. Got thrown trying to bust a bronc. I got a damn good hunch there ain't no use looking further for the Circle W foreman."

"But why?" Ethan asked. "And who?"

"Can't say, but I just got some information I think you'll find mighty interesting." Will Bridges had a smug look on his face that told Ethan the old lawman was bursting with news.

"What kind of information, Will?"

"Well, it was your idea. You asked me to check out the bank records with Clyde."

"Yes."

The sheriff pointed to the sheath of papers on his desk. "Clyde wrote up what he had on Jake Harper. But it wasn't so much what Clyde had, as it was what he didn't have."

Ethan had to restrain himself from prodding the sheriff to get to the end of his tale.

"It seems Jake quit doing business with the bank about six months back. He marched in one day and paid off his mortgage —it was better than a thousand dollars at the time—with a draft from a Cheyenne bank. He closed out his account with

Lockwood State, and Clyde never saw him again after that day."

"Did he say where he got the money or why he was closing out the account?"

"Said he got an inheritance but didn't say who from. He didn't act like he was mad or nothing, just said he decided to do his banking in Cheyenne."

"There's nothing unusual about that," Ethan said. "I have an account both here and in Cheyenne. Most cattlemen do. It's convenient since they sell cattle there."

"I don't argue that, Ethan. But, you see, I got Clyde to go a step further for us. I had him telegraph the Cheyenne bank and ask for information on new accounts belonging to either Jacob Harper or Cynthia Harper, or both. Clyde's banker friend wired back right pronto. That's where things get damned curious. Jake Harper had an account there with better than six thousand dollars in it."

Ethan whistled. "That's a lot of money. Jake Harper had some inheritance, if that's where it came from."

"That ain't the half of it," the sheriff said. "There was another account."

"Another?"

"Yep. Not in the name of Cynthia Harper, but in the joint names of Cynthia Harper Richards and Grant Richards," he grinned. "Well, what do you make of that?"

Ethan was struck speechless. Suddenly, some things were beginning to make sense. "It doesn't look like Cynthia Harper was going to have a child out of wedlock after all. You know what we got to do, Will?"

The sheriff grunted. "Yeah, we've got to go calling on the Webbs. And I'd sure as hell rather take a whipping. Old Gid's been a good friend—not just to me but to the whole town. Do you think I ought to deputize some men?"

"I don't see why. We're just going out to talk. As a lawyer, I'd have to say the evidence is still pretty flimsy. It's nothing but a guess who killed the Harpers. And everybody who can tie either of the Webbs directly to the killings is dead. Besides, Webb isn't apt to try anything on his home place."

"You know, I can't just accuse a man," the sheriff said.

"No, but you've got a right to ask questions. If you want, I'll do most of the talking. I've got some ideas, if you'll play along."

"The only idea I've got is retirement," the sheriff said. "I'll be more than glad to let you deal."

33

THE CIRCLE W ranch house was a sprawling, imposing structure built with logs hewn from the ponderosa that cloaked the surrounding hills. It was a county showplace as was the entire ranch complex that included a bunk house, two large barns, granary and other assorted outbuildings, and a maze of corrals and holding pens. It was a rancher's dream, Ethan thought, as he sat astride his rented mare and looked out over the Circle W's home base in the valley below.

The Circle W dwarfed Ethan's own Lazy R which adjoined a portion of Webb's land on the west, and which Gideon Webb would, no doubt, like to add to his own empire. On the other hand, perhaps he would someday add the Circle W to the Lazy R. It was a dream worth working for.

He smiled to himself. Was he really so different from Gideon Webb? Where would his own quest for empire lead him? Would he leave his values behind somewhere along the road? He liked to think not, but maybe Webb thought that way once, too.

He turned to the sober-faced sheriff on the horse beside him. "Well, I guess there's nothing to gain by waiting."

"I suppose not, but I sure got cold feet for such a hot day. Gid and me go back a long ways."

As they headed their horses down the road toward the ranch house, Ethan noticed that word of their visit had evidently preceded them. A half dozen cowhands were scattered about the house and outbuildings, trying too hard to look casual. The Circle W hands should have been busy in the hayfields or riding the range looking for strays on a day like this.

They moved slowly down the road that snaked its way to the valley where it leveled off and sliced through the greenest, lushest meadows in Wyoming, before it led into the Webb ranch headquarters.

The cowhands watched silently and warily as Ethan and Will Bridges dismounted and led their horses the remainder of the distance to the ranch house. Ethan took solace in the fact that the men stationed there were not professional guns. They were cowboys, pure and simple. He recognized most of them by sight, if not by name. They were loyal to their boss and benefactor and would kill for him in defense of life or property. But it was not likely they would be willing parties to murder or stand by and let it happen.

He spied Joe Hollings, the young cowboy he had bailed out of Will Bridges' jail, standing on the front porch with his hands shoved in his hip pockets. He looked uncomfortable as hell, possibly fretting about some of the things he had divulged to Enos Fletcher.

"Hello, Joe," Ethan said as he tied his horse to the hitching post.

Joe smiled nervously, and his face turned red as a ripe tomato. "Uh, howdy, Mr. Ramsey."

"How's it going, Joe? I haven't seen you for a spell."

Hollings glanced uneasily at his comrades. "Uh, fine, Mr. Ramsey. Ain't been in the hoosegow since that time last year. Sheriff can swear to that. I decided me and the bottle just don't mix."

Ethan moved closer to the porch. "It's a decision you won't regret, Joe. Say, are you still keeping company with that blonde gal? Sally Winter, isn't it?"

The scarlet that had started to fade, rushed back. "Yeah," he grinned. "We're getting hitched this fall."

"That's great, Joe. There's nothing like a good woman to steady a man. I know her family. They're good people. Congratulations to you."

"Thanks, Mr. Ramsey." The young man kept his eyes on Ethan, obviously trying to avoid the hostile stares that were being sent his way by the other cowboys.

Ethan felt badly about singling Joe Hollings out from the others, but he thought it was wise to seek an ally just in case things took a nasty turn.

"What can I do for you, Mr. Ramsey?" Joe asked.

"The sheriff and I came to see Mr. Webb . . . the senior Mr. Webb."

Hollings stepped onto the porch and rapped softly on the door. "I'll ask if he can see you."

Hollings rapped only twice before the heavy wooden door creaked open and a tall, lean man with thick wiry hair, the color of fresh mountain snow, stepped out. His sun-bronzed face was impassive as he studied Ethan with deep-set blue eyes for several moments before he turned to the sheriff. Ethan could understand why Katherine Wyeth would have been enamored by Gideon

Webb. As Skye had said, there was a magnetism in his bearing. And his white hair was the only hint of his advanced years.

"Good afternoon, Will," Webb said pleasantly enough. "It's been a spell. What brings you here?"

"I'm afraid it's not a social call, Gid. Mr. Ramsey and me came to palaver about all the trouble we've had in the valley since Jake Harper and young Cynthia were killed."

"Well, I don't know what good I can do you, Will, but you're welcome to come in and talk."

Ethan and the sheriff followed Gideon Webb into the house, but as they stepped inside, Ethan saw that Webb had not been alone in the house. A bulkier, taller version of the rancher, dressed like a dandy in hand-tooled black boots and an embroidered shirt, stood by the stone fireplace at the far end of the room. The young man had a sullen look, and his lips were frozen in a scowl as he eyed Ethan with contempt.

"Hello, Will," Clete Webb said without taking his eyes off Ethan.

The sheriff nodded, "Clete."

"Are you acquainted with my son, Mr. Ramsey?" Gideon Webb asked.

"We met a few days back at the Cottonwood Palace." Ethan noted with mild satisfaction that Clete, as did Ethan, still bore the marks of their meeting.

"Have a chair," Gideon said as he gestured with a wave of his hand to a horseshoe of plush, cowhide-covered chairs. "Can I get you some whiskey, Will?"

Ethan was not included in the offer.

"No. This ain't a whiskey-drinking visit."

As Gideon Webb took a chair on the opposite side of the

bearskin rug that separated him from Will Bridges, Ethan's eyes swept the spacious room. Clean plastered walls and an enormous fireplace constructed of rose granite. Huge, beamed ceilings carved from Missouri oak. Fine paintings on the walls. The house was indeed a showplace, but it was also functional. It was a home made to endure for generations as a monument to its founder.

"I'm listening, Will," Webb said. "What have you got to say?" His voice was not hostile, but it was not friendly, either.

The sheriff tossed an uneasy glance at Clete who had remained standing next to the fireplace. "We've been friends for a long time, Gid, and none of this makes sense to me, but all the killing and trouble we've had since the Harpers were killed point to the Circle W. I ain't accusing anybody—not yet—but me and Ethan came here looking for answers."

"I'm afraid I don't understand what Mr. Ramsey has to do with this," Webb said, casting Ethan a look of disdain.

"I'd be happy to explain, Mr. Webb," Ethan said. "You see, I'm Skye dePaul's lawyer. You'll recall she paid a visit to your ranch several days ago."

Webb's lips curved down slightly at the corners, but otherwise he appeared unshaken. He took a cigar out of his coat pocket, pressed it to his lips, lit it and inhaled deeply. Then he removed the cigar from his mouth and looked at it reflectively before he exhaled a thick plume of smoke.

"I presume you don't deny Miss dePaul visited here?"

Webb's eyes seemed to turn ice blue, and he replied coldly. "Ramsey, I don't have to answer your goddamn questions. You may be a lawyer, but you're not the law." He turned to the sheriff. "If there's to be any talking, Will, it'll be with you."

The sheriff shifted uncomfortably in his chair. Ethan

persisted. "No, you don't have to talk to me, Mr. Webb, but I know all about you—everything you've done—and I'll take it to a court of law, if that's the way you want it. But when it's in court, it's public record, and that makes it fair game for the newspapers. I think you'd rather hear it now than read about it."

Ethan saw Clete's hand inching toward his six-gun. "Think hard before you go for your gun, Clete," Ethan warned evenly. "You can't get by with killing a sheriff."

"Pa, goddamn it," Clete whined, "you going to let him come here and talk like that to us?"

"Shut up, Clete," his father snapped. Webb's face had paled noticeably, and the cigar trembled slightly in his fingers. "Mr. Ramsey, I think you're farting in the wind, but I'm a prominent man in this state, and I'm fair game for the press. I don't want our good name soiled by irresponsible charges, so I'll hear you out. If you have questions, perhaps I can clarify things for you."

"Back to Miss dePaul, then," Ethan said. "Will you acknowledge that she paid a visit to the Circle W?"

"Yes, I believe she stopped by here."

"She asked you about something she found at the Harper place, isn't that right, Mr. Webb?"

He rubbed his chin thoughtfully. "Yes, I believe so, but she was very irrational, and I didn't get her point."

"Perhaps I can help you. The sheriff and I picked this up at the Harper place." Ethan reached into his coat pocket and pulled out a tarnished gold watch. "Miss dePaul said she told you she found a watch in the ashes, Mr. Webb. This watch. Do you recognize it?"

Ethan caught a flicker of panic in Webb's eyes. The astonished look on Clete's face told Ethan that Gideon Webb's son recognized the timepiece. "It has the Circle W brand engraved on the case," Ethan said. "I'd say that would give us good reason to look here for the owner, wouldn't you?"

"I don't know what you're driving at, Ramsey."

"Miss dePaul told you about finding this watch, and after she left this ranch, some gunslingers chased her into the mountains and tried to kill her. They almost got the job done. As it is, she lost an arm. But I expect you've already heard."

Webb was noncommittal. "A most attractive young woman. Tragic. Very tragic."

"How do you explain your watch being at the Harper's?"

"My watch?"

"That's what I said."

Webb tugged at the watch chain that was suspended across the front of his vest. "My watch is right here."

"I'm certain that a man of your means has more than one watch, Mr. Webb. But let me explain further. Cynthia tore this watch from her killer while she struggled for her life. A struggle she lost. A cowhand wouldn't wear a watch like this, Mr. Webb. If he did, it would be stuffed deep in his front pocket. A man like yourself, though, wears his watch where it's easy to grab." Ethan saw the animal fear in Gideon's eyes and read the truth there. The gamble had paid off.

"Ethan," Will Bridges said, a perplexed look on his face, "what are you saying?"

"I know what he's saying," Clete roared. "Pa, you can't let him get away with that. He's trying to say you killed Cynthia and her pa. Let me take care of the son-of-a-bitch."

"Shut your mouth," Webb said. "Ramsey, you're bluffing. I'm not a lawyer, but I know enough to be damn sure that what you just said isn't evidence. It's just speculation."

"Maybe, but I have evidence, and the law's going to turn up more when I lay it all out. I'll tell you something, Mr. Webb. I'm sure enough of what I've got that I'll just show you all my cards. I assume you remember a gentleman by the name of Ramon Sanchez? He was on your ranch payroll. We can find a half dozen ranch hands outside to testify to that. I killed Sanchez, but before he died, he told me you were the one who sent him to kill Skye dePaul. That's enough to cause you a lot of trouble. At first, I thought that didn't prove anything about who killed the Harpers." Ethan looked up at Clete who appeared numb with shock. "In fact, I thought Clete had killed the Harpers. I could think of a half dozen possible motives. I figured you were just trying to protect your son. Inexcusable, but not unnatural. None of the pieces of that puzzle seemed to fit, though. Then it hit me this morning and everything came together, and now I know how it happened. Want me to tell you?"

Webb snuffed out his cigar in an ashtray and leaned back in his chair, his head drooping in resignation. "I'm not admitting to anything, but I'll listen to your story."

"The remains of Grant Richards were found in the rubble of what would have been a bedroom in the Harper house. Dr. Weintraub can testify that he was shot in the back of the head. The broken leg Richards once had provides reasonable identification of the body. I think you killed him with his own Smith & Wesson .44. You must have found it hanging in the parlor when you entered the house. Cynthia was there when you killed him, and she tried to get away. I don't know why you didn't shoot her. Maybe you caught her as she was escaping through the bedroom door, and it was just more convenient to strangle her. I think Jake showed up unexpectedly after you killed Cynthia. That's why they were both in the front room. Feel free to correct me if I'm wrong."

"I was playing poker at Langford's that night, Ramsey, and a half dozen men can attest to that."

We can establish that the killings took place sometime between seven thirty and nine o'clock, and we'll be able to pin it down closer. I doubt if your game started that early, and in any case, Charley Langford should be able to tell us about when you got to his place. I'd guess you went straight from the Harpers' to your alibi."

Webb's face had turned to stone. Ethan looked up at Clete again.

"Cynthia was carrying a child. She was secretly married to Grant Richards; we don't know when the two got married, but we'll find out soon enough."

Clete slumped down to the floor and buried his face in his hands and began to whimper. "Pa, why? Why?"

"I can answer that," Ethan said. "Somehow, your father learned that Grant Richards and his father-in-law had been rustling Circle W cattle for the past year. You know better than anyone, Clete, how your father felt about Grant Richards. Betrayal. Most men are lucky if they have one, maybe two persons they can place absolute trust in during their lifetimes. It's hard for a man to trust, especially one like your father. When you do, and you find it was misplaced, it does something to you." He turned back to Webb. "You should know, Mr. Webb, that we located bank accounts belonging to Richards and Harper. From there, we should be able to trace the source of the money. That establishes motive. A lawyer would call the evidence circumstantial, but if there's enough of it, it can hang a man. There will be, now that we know what we're looking for. I'm sorry for you, Mr. Webb. After seeing what you've accomplished and all the good you've done, it's sad that it has come to this. But I'm sorrier yet, for all the people you left in your trail of blood. Harper and Richards had something coming for what they did, but not death. Cynthia and her unborn child. Ben Dobbs. Skye dePaul. Two innocent Indian boys. Clete still has to answer for his part in that."

Webb spoke, his voice strangely firm and detached. "Grant came to me that day, said he was quitting, that there wasn't any future in the ranch because when I died, Clete would boot him off the place before I was six feet under. I asked him where he was going, what he was going to do. That's when he told me he'd married Cynthia Harper six months back. He said Jake was going to sell his spread, and they had their eyes on a place in Colorado. Damn, it was a kick in the balls. He left me sick when he walked out. Then I got to thinking about it . . . the rustling stopped when the hired guns showed up. Grant Richards was the first to know when I made the decision to get help. I remember he was against it at first; we had our biggest losses in the days just before the gunmen arrived. And where would Grant Richards and Harper get the money to invest in a Colorado ranch? Between them they didn't have as much as a desert grasshopper. I had been blind to it because I was always blind where Grant was concerned. I saw that all at once. I wasn't about to let him get away with it . . . not Grant. I didn't give a shit about Jake Harper. I would have been willing to let the law take care of him. And Cynthia . . . it was just her hard luck to be there when I went to the Harper place to find Grant. They were in the bedroom, the two of them. I could have used my own gun, but I saw his gun belt hanging by the door. It would be ironic, I thought, if I killed him with the same gun I gave him. So I did. He was bare-ass naked and asleep when I put the bullet in the back of his head. I regretted that I didn't see his eyes, that he never knew that I paid him off in full. The rest of it was pretty much as you said, except for a few details. Cynthia had been getting dressed and tried to get away. I fired a wild shot and missed, but I caught her and couldn't let her go. I had never struck a woman in my life, much less killed one. It was a degrading thing to do."

"I'm going to have to take you in, Gid," Will Bridges said, his voice raspy. "I didn't know that when we came here. I thought Clete, maybe, but I never saw it was you. I guess I had my blind spot, too."

"You've got your job to do, Will. I don't hold it against you. It's all over; I won't be any trouble." He rose from his chair. "Will you trust me to pack a few things?"

Bridges looked uncertainly at Ethan who shrugged. "Yeah, sure, I guess. You're not going to shoot your way out of this one."

Gideon smiled. "You never know, old partner, you never know." He walked over to Clete who was huddled against the wall, sobbing like a small child. He stood over his son for a moment and opened his mouth as if to say something. He then shook his head as if he thought better of it. He trudged toward the open doorway of a room Ethan assumed was a bedroom. Fifteen minutes had aged Webb twenty years, he thought. Gideon Webb was a man who was on his way to dying.

No sooner had the thought passed through Ethan's mind, than the gunshot roared in the next room.

34

SKYE WALKED INTO his office unannounced, and taken aback, Ethan scrambled out of his chair to greet her. She acknowledged him with a slight nod and took a chair on the opposite side of his desk.

She was dressed in the same Quaker garb she had been wearing that first day she marched into his office. She looked much the same—proud, defiant, her face a bit stern. She was lovely in spite of the gauntness of her face and the noticeable hollowness about her eyes. Time would remedy that. The pinned-back sleeve that covered her left arm would always be that way.

"You look a bit foolish standing there like that, Ethan," she said. "I suggest you be seated."

He dropped into his chair. "I wasn't expecting you. Henry said he wouldn't be releasing you for a few more days."

"I released myself." She reached into the bosom of her dress and withdrew an envelope which she handed to him. "There is a draft in the envelope for another three hundred dollars," she said, "to be applied to the fees I owe you. If you can advise me of the balance, I shall make arrangements for payment."

He pushed the envelope back to her side of the desk. "I don't want more fees. I wouldn't feel right about it. I didn't even perform any real legal services."

She ignored his gesture. "You performed the services I employed you to perform. You are well paid with the additional three hundred dollars, but I want nothing of your charity."

"Damn it, it's not charity."

"Ethan, please do not be unpleasant."

"Who's being unpleasant? It's just that this had become more than a case to me. That is, you and me . . . I thought—"

"I am leaving later this morning, Ethan. Now that Clete Webb has been arrested and the few leaders of the lynch mob who are not already dead are in custody, I am returning to my people."

"What?"

"I am going to the village of my uncle."

"That's ridiculous. That's not where your life is. You belong here. Besides, you're in no condition to ride into those mountains alone. At least let me go with you. I've taken Joe Hollings on at the ranch, and he'll look after things there."

"I am well enough for the journey, and Bear Killer will be with me. It was my wish to thank you personally before I left, for all you have done for my people . . . and for me."

She was saying good-bye. What possessed this crazy woman? Didn't she know how he felt? Had he deluded himself about her feelings for him? Talons of despair clutched his heart. For some days now he had been unable to envision a life that did not include Skye dePaul.

He looked into the dark, limpid pools that were her eyes and saw the sadness there. There did not have to be words between him and Skye for them to speak to each other. She was telling him now that she cared, felt what he felt. Then why say good-bye?

"Skye," he said, "stay with me."

"Please, Ethan, do not make it difficult," she said, as she rose from her chair. "I must go now."

He got up and moved quickly around his desk, blocking her escape. "You can't leave until I ask you something." Again their eyes locked.

"Do not ask it now, Ethan, for I cannot give you the answer you wish."

"But what about the prophecy? The coyote?"

"I am a civilized Indian, Ethan. I do not believe in such things."

To his relief, though, she qualified her answer.

"If the vision carried any truth, perhaps the prophecy has already been fulfilled, and you have made more of it than there was. If there is more to unfold, it will happen in its own way, in its own time." She suddenly stepped toward him and brushed her lips softly against his cheek before pushing past him and hurrying out the door.

He fought off the urge to follow. "Not now," he muttered to himself, "not now." He walked dejectedly back to the desk and stood beside it, staring at the sealed envelope for some moments before he picked it up and opened it. He took out the draft, gave it a cursory glance, and tossed it on his desk and sunk into his chair, turning his attention to the will he had been working on before his interruption. Then he picked up the draft and looked at it again. His eyes were not playing tricks on him. It was definitely not signed. An oversight? Should he go after her? She would no doubt be stopping off at the Pennock School to change before heading into the mountains. No, he reminded himself, not now.

In a few weeks, before July faded into August, the mountains would offer a cool respite from the baking oven of Lockwood. It might be just the right time to ride up to Lame Buffalo's village to get Skye's signature on the draft.

58519440R00145

Made in the USA
Lexington, KY
12 December 2016